VAMPIRE CITY COVEN
TROLL VILLAGE
WEREWOLF CITY
DARK FEY TERRITORY
WITCH LANDS
LIGHT FEY CITY
WOLF GIRL SERIE

I GRIPPED the steering wheel of my 1968 Beetle while Liv sobbed in the seat next to me. I had just told her that Sterling was killed and that I'd found his head in a box at Riverfront Park. Now I was following a black stretch limousine which carried *Prince* Luka and his betrothed into Vampire City.

"It's my fault." Liv wiped her tears on the back of her hand. "It was my idea to involve him."

We'd all grown up together. Sterling was like a brother to Liv. This was a pain that would take a while to heal. I was too numb to feel anything right now. I still had to tell her that we had no money and weren't entirely human. But now didn't seem like the best time for that.

"No, Liv. We both made the decision to tell Sterling, and he made his own choices too."

Maybe that wasn't totally truthful, but it was the only thing getting me through this drive.

"That poisonous bitch!" Liv screamed suddenly. "I loved her!"

Maz.

The numbness fled my body, quickly replaced with a pulse of anger so strong I thought I might snap the steering wheel right off.

"We *all* loved her," I growled. "Believed in her." I wanted to turn this car right around and drive back to the society so that I could take her head clean off.

Liv chewed on her lip. "I mean, are we sure it was her…?"

I sighed. I guess now was as good a time as any. Reaching into the back seat, I retrieved the manilla envelope Sterling had sent me and handed it to her.

"Start with his letter to me," I told her.

She frowned, taking the papers out and finding the handwritten letter. Small gasps came from her mouth one after the other and she reached out to squeeze my leg in support. "Our money is gone?" she asked.

"Yes. I checked," was all I said.

She lifted off the letter and went through the papers. My heart jackknifed in my chest. I should have said something, I should have maybe just verbally told her, but I was too much of a coward. Or maybe I wanted her to find out the same way I did, so I could see what conclusions she came to. So that I could make sure I wasn't crazy, that I hadn't jumped to the wrong conclusions.

Gasp after gasp tore from her throat until finally her hand covered her mouth. "I feel sick."

My heart shattered. Watching someone you love go through a pain and shock you couldn't take from them, it cut deep. Soul deep.

"Yeah … I had a similar reaction."

"We're not … fully human? We were bought like *slaves*?" There was disbelief in her voice as she pulled back and looked at her hands as if expecting to see fey magical powers come out of them.

I just nodded, comforted that we'd come to the same conclusions.

"And Maz signed off on it!" she growled, her fists clenching.

I knew there was nothing I could say, so I stayed quiet over the next hour as she ranged between venting and screaming. Finally, she just leaned her head against the glass in a numb catatonic state.

Liv. My sweet sister, best friend. I wanted to console her, but I was in the same depressed and disbelieving state, so all I could do was be there as we both processed this new reality together.

We'd already crossed the border into Idaho, and

now made our way past Coeur d'Alene and up the US-95 toward Bonners Ferry.

When the limo pulled off at an unmarked exit, I followed. I hadn't really paid attention the last time I'd been in Magic City. I'd been flown in under sedation and Sage and Walsh had driven me out in a barely conscious state. Now that I was paying attention, I saw that there was a weird shimmer to the air on the far right, like a dome or bubble. We turned off the main road and onto a dirt road in the direction of the shimmering tree line. After a long winding road through the thick forest, we came upon a giant wrought iron gate.

There was a man sitting there, on a chair in the middle of nowhere, reading a book. He looked human, but now I wondered. As Luka's limo approached, the man put down his book and stepped over to peer inside their car. I looked at the man more closely, the way he walked, the paleness to his skin.

Vampire.

I had that involuntary inward cringe and then chastised myself. It would take a while before the mental conditioning I'd been exposed to all my life wore down. He was a vampire, yes, but that didn't mean he was evil.

The limo pulled through the gates and then he

waved us inside as well without so much as a second glance. Luka must have told him he needed his *feeder.*

That bastard. "I can't believe he's engaged and didn't tell me."

Liv shrugged. "Who cares … unless." She spun on me. "You totally like him!"

I winced. "I mean, he's charming and sexy, so yeah he got to me for a hot minute, but I'm over him."

She grinned. "He got to you how?"

"Shut up."

"You kissed him!" She pointed an accusing finger at me. "Holy crap, you kissed a bloodsucker."

I rolled my eyes, my cheeks heating up at the memory. "One kiss. It wasn't a big deal."

Liv stared at the rolling green hills and thick trees as a city in the distance grew larger. "Does this mean we don't have to stay virgins?" she queried.

I chuckled. "I don't know. I still think it would be nice to wait until my wedding night. Save it for the guy I'm going to spend the rest of my life with." She had a point though … I think what made me the maddest was that Maz used God to control us. My relationship with the creator was an important thing to me. Praying brought me comfort, helping others gave me joy, vanquishing evil in God's name was my purpose. But Maz distorted all that with the *Hunter Scriptures,* handpicked verses from the Bible that proved our cause was to hunt the demons of this earth.

For we wrestle not against flesh and blood, but against principalities, against powers, against the rulers of the darkness of this world, against spiritual wickedness in high places. Ephesians 6:12

Maz had built an entire religion on that one line in the bible … a book that was supposed to be read in its entirety and not cherry picked to fit her narrative.

I am such an idiot, I thought.

I'd never even read the entire Bible, but I knew the *Hunter Scriptures* by heart. Shame burned deep inside of me as I warred with my own spiritual collapse and what this meant for my beliefs.

"Holy crap," Liv breathed. "Is that Vampire City?"

Tossing my inner turmoil aside, I followed her gaze. "Whoa."

I hadn't expected it to be so … old. It was beautiful, but didn't feel like it should be in the middle of Northern Idaho. Gothic spires shot up from the tops of stone cathedrals. Smaller buildings dotted the landscape, but at the very top of the hill there was a giant castle with a stone wall surrounding it. Outside the wall sat many other stone outbuildings, all with the same Old World European look.

There were no farmlands, just rolling green hills and trees, and then I remembered vampires didn't need food, they drank only blood. A small village off to the east had some more modern looking houses and I wondered if that's where they kept their feeders. We passed through a village but there weren't many people out and about. Cute, old English-looking cottages dotted the village roadside. It was odd to see a brand-new Mercedes parked along an old cobblestone road. Vampire City reminded me of Rome—not that I'd ever been, but I'd seen pictures of it.

We reached another set of gates at the high stone wall surrounding the castle. They let Luka's limousine through, but this time had me roll down the window to speak with someone.

"Hello, Miss Rose. Luka has requested that you and your sister be brought to his guest quarters on his estate while he attends a meeting."

I just nodded. I was too tired to care about anything right now. A man dressed in a suit, who resembled some type of butler, suddenly appeared before us in a black golf cart and waved for me to follow.

I pulled through and the giant white stone castle

rose up to an incredible height as I drove around the back of it to a smaller house. There was a stone sign in front that said *Drake Guest Cottage II*.

I shivered. That Drake name was synonymous with murder, rape, and all things evil. I had a hard time believing that Luka was from such a wicked family.

The butler dude pulled into a little space in front of the cottage and I parked to the side of him. After getting out and grabbing our duffle bags, Liv and I walked across the simple yet beautiful garden and into the open front door of the small home. All vestiges of Old World vibes were gone the moment we entered the home. Dry wall had been put up over the stone and there were granite counters, flat screen TV's and all the modern comforts you could ask for. The furniture was plush and comfortable in creams and grays.

The butler stepped inside and turned to face us, bowing deeply.

He wasn't a vampire, that much was clear. From the tips of his pointy ears I would suspect he was fey or at least part. Now that I knew that was a thing…

"Good afternoon, ladies, my name is Gunner and I will be at your service during your stay here."

We both waved at him awkwardly.

He gestured to the flat screen TV. "On your TV,

you will find an app called *Home Assistant,* from which you can order food, house cleaning, medical and emergency assistance. You can even call me directly." He held out his phone. "Anything you want, I will bring to you."

Whoa. Okay, that might be cool.

"Burger King?" Liv raised an eyebrow.

He nodded. "There is one in Coeur d'Alene. I can have it for you within thirty minutes."

Liv grinned. "I'll take a bacon whopper with cheese and onion rings."

He tapped something on his phone and looked at me expectantly. "And for you, miss?"

Okay … I could definitely get used to this. "The same. Thanks."

"Shoot wait, we don't have any money," I added. It was going to take some time for it to settle in that I was suddenly broke.

Gunner looked nonplussed. "Everything is paid for by the crown. You're feeders to a prince. It's a very important job."

Feeders? Plural? So that's how he got Liv in here?

"In that case, can you add two strawberry milk-shakes," Liv said.

He nodded. "Of course, my lady. Anything else?"

Liv shrugged. "Think that's all for now. Do you have Netflix?"

She dropped her hunter bag and walked into the living room.

Gunner inclined his head. "The TV is equipped with all of the channels and shows that humans like."

We aren't exactly human anymore ... weird thought. Did vampires not like TV? That was even weirder. Maybe they thought they were too good for TV, like it rotted your brain.

"I'll take my leave, then, if that's all? The food will be here shortly," he said.

I murmured my thanks and he bowed before leaving, closing the door behind him.

"This is weird," I told Liv.

"This is awesome!" she said as she scrolled through the movies with her feet up on the couch. "I find out I'm suddenly broke and ten minutes later I'm a sugar baby to a rich vampire prince."

I snort-laughed. "I don't think Luka is old enough to be a sugar daddy."

"Whatever. Let's stay here however long he will let us." She stopped on a teen drama and clicked the play button.

Leaving Liv to veg out on the couch, I did a quick tour of the place. It was a three-bedroom guest home, with two bathrooms, a cute little kitchen off the living room, and a formal dining room off the front entryway. So Luka must be sleeping in the castle. With Cassara…

I slumped into a chair in the living room and stared aimlessly at the TV, not really paying attention for the next hour.

Liv was good at turning her brain off in times of stress. She was already into the fifth episode of some new show, our burgers long eaten, when there was a knock at the door. I knew who it was even before I answered. I sensed him.

Luka.

I cleared my throat. "I'll get it."

What the hell did he want? He'd already fed this morning and he was high as a kite if he thought he was feeding twice a day now just because he was a king in training or whatever.

I yanked the door back with a growl in my throat, still bitter about that kiss and finding out about his fiancée. "You better not be asking for a second meal so soo—"

I jerked to a stop when I saw the blood seeping through the front of his shirt, the paleness of his skin, and the weary look in his eye.

"Crap, Luka." I rushed forward as he staggered into me. "What happened?"

My heart softened as I took in the state of him.

He stumbled inside, leaning on me for support as

I veered him into the dining room and sat him down. He winced with each movement, more blood pooling at his abdomen.

"Luka, you need a doctor." I gaped at him as he casually extended his legs out from the chair and leaned back with a pained expression on his face. He was covered in blood and ash. He looked like he'd just come back from a war.

"I'm fine," he stated, grabbing at his right side. "I broke away the moment I could because I wanted to explain a few things to you. About Cassara and… everything." His face was marred with guilt and it kind of blew me away. I hadn't expected him to address everything—especially not while he was bleeding!

"Okay… but maybe you could like, not die first? We can talk later." I waved him off, trying to act like I didn't care about the whole Cassara thing.

His hand snaked out, grasping mine and holding it tenderly. "Aspen Rose, I am a man of *honor*. If I date two women at once, I let them know about it beforehand."

I chuckled, rolling my eyes. "Is this supposed to be an apology? Because you're failing."

A sly grin swept across his face before becoming serious. "What I mean is… I've never had a kiss like that before in my life." He sat up straighter, grimacing at the apparent pain as he leaned closer to me. "And I would *never* hide a woman from you. I didn't know Cassara was still alive and that our… arrangement… still stood."

A lump formed in my throat. "It's fine," I said too quickly.

Luka shook his head slowly, side to side. "It's *not* fine, and I'm going to find a way to fix it … somehow. Because I want more kisses like that." He leaned into me and sniffed my neck, dragging his lips against my throat, which caused my heart to pound wildly in my chest.

Fix it? Fix his arranged marriage to Cassara? How? Why? Because of one kiss?

I pulled back from him, swallowing hard. "Maybe it's for the best."

His brows drew together to form a knot between his eyes. "That I marry Cassara?"

I nodded, swallowing hard as bile rose in my throat. The thought of seeing him marry another woman made me sick, and that reaction scared the shit out of me. Why did I care? I barely knew this guy…

But was that really true? I'd argue that I'd never known someone more intimately. Our bond was to thank for that. Even now I felt the hurt slice through him at my words.

"You're a bad liar," he snarled, standing and swaying on his feet.

I caught him by the elbow and he glared at me.

"Luka, stop being stubborn and see a damn doctor!" I yanked the hem of his shirt up and gasped when I saw two giant slashes across his abdomen. They were weeping clear-ish pink fluid. Healing, but slowly.

"Holy hell, what happened?"

His yellow eyes were burning into me with a hunger that I didn't think had anything to do with blood. "I got in a fight," he stated plainly.

I crossed my arms, glaring him down. "If being king is going to get you killed, maybe you should rethink your plans. You don't seem like the type to want to be in charge anyway."

He sighed, shaking his head. "There is nothing I would like more than to light a match to this shithole and watch it all burn, but too many people are depending on me." A darkness crossed his features and I frowned.

"What do you mean?"

"Oh, you care now?" he snapped.

Bastard!

"I'm here, aren't I? I haven't let you starve, have I?"

He leveled me with his gaze. "Remember Walsh?"

I nodded. "The werewolf."

He bobbed his head in confirmation. "He's the one who killed the vampire king last year, my uncle."

My mouth popped open. That had been such big news at the Vampire Hunter Society. "Wait, I heard he was jailed."

"He was. He was jailed so that his best friend Sawyer wouldn't be alone."

Wow, that was what I called a good friend.

"What did Sawyer do to go to jail?" I mean, now that we were digging into history, I might as well get my questions answered.

"He killed Vicon Drake, the king's son and prince of Vampire City. Because Vicon raped his wife, Demi."

My hand flew to my mouth as my heart twisted in my chest. Vicon raped Demi? *Holy crap.* This further cemented the knowledge I had that most vampires were absolute dirtbags and deserved to die!

"And now I need to become king and pardon Walsh, or the Magical Creature Council will find him and lock him away for life. He won't survive in Magic City Prison. Not without his crew. We..." A darkness passed over his features. "We kept each other alive in there."

Five Crew. I couldn't imagine being locked up in a

prison full of supernaturals without Liv or anyone else I knew to get my back. Unexpected tears welled in my eyes and my bitterness at Luka softened. "Then I guess we better make you king. How many others do you have to defeat? Nine?" He'd said ten competitors total.

He grinned, pointing to the wound at his stomach. "Seven now."

My mouth popped open in surprise. "Oh."

Luka looked over at me, and I stared back at him. We just drank each other in, not speaking a word for a full minute. In another world, one where I hadn't been bred to hate vampires and one where he wasn't engaged … we might have been something amazing.

I could feel emotions swirling between us, their depth unfathomable.

That kiss, that kiss we shared back in his apartment … we were both thinking of it.

I drew in a shaky breath, wondering what my future would be like. Him married to Cassara while he snuck away to feed from me…?

"I—" he started as I cleared my throat.

I cut him off. "It's getting late. I'm tired." It had been a whirlwind of a few days and I just wanted to lie in bed and go to sleep. I wanted to properly mourn Sterling and the fact that I wasn't even human. None of which Luka knew, and now I wasn't even sure how or why I should tell him such a thing. Even though we were bonded, the closeness I felt to him evaporated the instant I saw Cassara.

Luka frowned but nodded and started for the door. I walked with him, happy to see that he seemed to be a bit better and his healing was kicking in. He must have literally run here the second he was free of his fight.

I opened the door and he turned to face me with a serious look. "No one must know you and I are bonded, that you alone are my feeder," he whispered into my ear. "It would put you at great risk and remove my ability to become future king."

I frowned.

"As far as people are concerned, you and Liv are *both* my feeders," he said sternly.

I nodded absentmindedly, confused by his earlier statement.

"Why would you having a bonded feeder remove your ability to become future king?" I whispered back, matching his volume.

A sadness crossed over his features then. "You haven't realized yet?"

My confusion deepened. "Realized what?"

Luka reached out and twirled a lock of my red hair between his fingers. "My lifespan is dictated by yours, Aspen. When you die, I will starve to death."

It was like I'd been socked in the stomach, the wind rushed out of me as an overwhelming grief tore through my chest.

"No," I breathed.

I hadn't even thought about that, I'd been so focused on hating him and the inconvenience this bond brought to *my* life, I never considered his. It must be a rule that a reigning king had to be immortal. I mean, obviously, wasn't that a basic tenet of being a vampire?

Leaning forward, he brushed his lips to my cheek. "It was worth it," he whispered before pulling back and walking away, leaving me a tornado of thoughts and feelings I couldn't even begin to deal with.

I TOSSED and turned all night, dreams of Sterling and Luka swirling around my mind. I finally woke in the early morning hours and, surprisingly, thought of Maz. What was she doing right now? Morning prayer walk? Was she looking for us? Or did she just give away our apartment and promote two hunters to replace us? Did she tell everyone we died, we ran? I wanted closure, answers—I wanted to knock the entire fake society on its ass—but I also wanted to know more about this breeder situation … my mother. And I needed to be here for Luka for the next month as agreed. Pushing all of these thoughts to the side, I decided while I was in Magic City I might as well try to enjoy it.

After showering and putting on some jeans and a t-shirt, I went out into the hallway and immediately heard hushed voices. I followed them into the kitchen and found Liv, Demi, and Sage all laughing about something. I was so surprised to see the two werewolves that I skidded to a stop and stared. Liv was acting all chummy with them, which was a relief as I liked both Demi and Sage. Even though the last time I'd seen them had been under strenuous conditions, I respected them a lot.

"Morning," I mumbled and they all looked up at me, still grinning.

Demi waved me over. "Hope you don't mind us crashing here a few days. Luka got us in so we could watch his fights, but we're posing as feeders so his biatch doesn't get suspicious that you're the only one."

I chuckled at her term for Cassara. "Werewolf feeders? An *alpha* feeder? Is anyone really going to believe that?" I doubted it.

Demi shrugged. "Vampires can feed from any race and they are kind of stupid. They won't recognize my scent with these on." She held up her wrists and I saw two metal cuffs there.

I frowned. "Those make them not recognize you?"

Sage rolled her eyes. "Okay, it's a long story, but here is the deal. Demi is a split shifter. Her wolf jumps out of her body like a ghost and can walk through walls and stuff. This makes her very powerful and her blood extra yummy and smell extra good, so the cuffs deaden her scent and power."

Demi glared at Sage. "Thank you for that eloquent explanation."

Sage shrugged, tossing her red hair over one shoulder. "It's too long of a story. I wanted to shorten it so we could move on to more important things like this." She shoved her hand in my direction and I stared at it confused.

Demi grinned. "Sage and Walsh got engaged, she's telling every soul she sees."

I focused and saw the small gold band on her ring finger and a grin pulled at my lips. "Congrats! That's so exciting." That must have been why they were all laughing and smiling when I walked in.

Sage did a little hip shimmy. "Wedding is going to be huge. You're both invited once Luka wins."

Once Luka wins … because Walsh was a wanted felon for killing the old vampire king. I was reminded of Luka's plight last night. Now I wanted him to win more than ever, even if only for Sage's happiness.

Liv and I both smiled. "Thanks, we will be there."

Werewolf wedding? Sure, why not. A month ago I wouldn't be caught dead at one, and now I was kind of excited. It was cool to just be a normal girl right now and let the past few days and stresses fade away.

"So Sawyer doesn't want to see Luka fight?" I grabbed an apple and took a bite, wondering why Demi's husband wasn't here.

Demi played with her blond hair and I noticed her t-shirt had a different saying today. *Leader of the pack.*

"That would be a problem with the vampire council. Technically, Sawyer killed Prince Vicon, and besides, we have a son, so he's home parenting while I get to have a week of girl time." She grinned.

I felt lighter by the moment. Maybe my time here wouldn't be too bad after all. A girls' week with two werewolves, what could go wrong?

We passed the day watching movies. I learned that Demi had grown up in Spokane at Delphi Academy as a banished wolf, but Sage had grown up in Werewolf City and they didn't have cable there apparently.

Sage pouted. "We must remedy this immediately! How do the vampires have *Teen Wolf* and we don't!"

I grinned and Demi nodded. "You're right. As a part of the rebuild, we are totally getting cable and internet laid throughout the city."

Sage reached out her hand and Demi high fived it.

Liv and I shared a smile. It was cute to see their close friendship. They acted like sisters, much like Liv and I. Liv stood up as the next episode started and motioned that I follow her to the dining room.

With a frown, I got up and left, turning the corner and meeting Liv in the more private area.

"What's up?" I whispered. "They're cool, right? You okay having them here?" I was totally fine among the two werewolves' presence, but now I wondered if I had misread Liv. Maybe she wasn't.

Liv shook her head. "No, it's not that. They are totally cool. I'm wondering if … while we are here, and they are here…" Her eyes widened.

I frowned, completely confused. "Spit it out, Livvie. I don't understand."

Liv dropped her voice. "Isn't it killing you that we are part fey and born to mothers in a breeding program that we know nothing about it? Maybe they do? Maybe … our moms are still alive? *Here.*"

Maybe our moms are still alive.

That single sentence flushed cold water through my veins; the hairs stood on the back of my neck. Why hadn't I even considered it? "You think … I mean…" I was at a loss for words.

"Demi told me that she and Sage have traveled all over Magic City. What if they know something that would help us find this breeding house or whatever?"

Holy crap, she was right. We could use our time here to find our moms!

"So we trust them?" I gulped.

Liv shrugged. "I think we have to if we want answers."

TWENTY MINUTES LATER, I'd told Sage and Demi everything. They just sat there quietly absorbing it all, reading Sterling's note and the attached papers, all of it. I held nothing back. When I'd told them about finding Sterling's head in a box, Demi reached out and clasped my hand in support.

"I knew your ears were a little too pointy!" Sage commented then. I laughed, nervously reaching up to touch them. Were they?

"Can you help us? Find our moms?" I asked.

Demi and Sage shared a look, one I couldn't interpret.

"The war is over," Demi said. "The werewolves and vampires are on thin ice until a new king is crowned. But there is a one constant enemy of my people and that's the Ithaki."

Ithaki. That was the word I'd forgotten. It was the word for…

"That's what you are," Sage said in a small voice. "The fey have magic that can cause them to be able to breed with any race, and the product of a fey mixed with anything is an Ithaki."

Demi nodded. "But mixing with humans is *so* forbidden it isn't even funny."

"But they did!" Liv growled angrily.

"So, we're the bad guys?" I frowned. I hadn't really expected to hear that. I was part of a race that was at odds with the werewolves? That felt weird now that I sat across from two of them.

"No, you're not bad," Demi added. "But most of the Ithaki are, and we are still at war with them, so it will be harder to help you but not impossible."

My heart lightened at that. "What are you saying?"

Demi and Sage shared a look and both nodded.

"I'm saying I like a challenge," said Demi, "and I have a friend who might know about the breeding program your moms are in."

"Who? Where are they? Can we go see them while we are here?" I was full of questions.

Demi nodded. "Her name is Marmal. She's a member of my pack. A troll."

Troll! I could feel my eyes widened. There was a troll in a wolfpack?

"When can we go?" I was excited to hear any news of my mom.

Demi shrugged. "Have you fed Luka today?"

I shook my head. "Not yet."

"Call him over, feed him, and we will go. You guys can come to Werewolf City and meet Marmal. I'll have her ready to talk." Demi said it so casually, like she wasn't arranging the most important meeting I'd ever have in my life.

If my mom was alive … what would I do? What would she say? The endless possibilities filled up my brain as Liv typed something on the fancy TV app Gunner had shown us.

"Luka has been summoned for lunch," Liv said, and I glared at her, although it wasn't untrue.

A mere few moments later there was a knock at the door. Demi answered it and Luka gave her a hug. "Hey, I got a text saying you guys were leaving the city and I needed to feed now or starve?" Luka sounded annoyed.

"Liv!" I yelled at my bestie, who grinned and shared a high five with Sage.

Demi snort-laughed. "Yeah, I'm taking the girls to Werewolf City for a tour. We will be back by nightfall."

Luka stepped into the space and his eyes searched for me. When they stopped on me sitting cross-legged on the floor, they burned yellow.

"No. She could be hurt," he said with finality.

My head reeled back at his abrupt dismissal, but Demi took it all in stride. "You're cute when you think you can tell us what to do."

Luka glared at her. "I'm in a fight for my life and you want to take my only feeder to our recent enemy's lands?"

Demi put a hand on her hip. "I'm the alpha of those lands, you dipshit. I'm not going to let anything happen to her! Besides, your next fight isn't for a few days, right?"

My lips pulled up into a smirk at her calling him a dipshit.

He shook his head, resigned. "You want to risk this just to sightsee? I find that hard to believe." His gaze fell on the manilla folder on the living room floor and the papers sprawled everywhere.

My cheeks reddened as I gathered them up quickly, hiding them from view.

'Wasn't that the folder you had back in Spokane and wanted to show me?' he asked in my mind. *'I totally forgot with all the ... drama.'*

Yeah, before he said he was engaged.

'Don't worry about it. Focus on your tournament or whatever. We will be back tonight. Promise.'

His brow furrowed. *'Are you in trouble, Aspen? You can tell me anything.'*

I shook my head. *'No. I'm fine.'* Technically, that wasn't a lie because I wasn't in trouble, but I felt far from fine.

Everyone in the room got really quiet, and I think it was obvious to them we were speaking mentally.

'What do the papers say?' His voice was gravelly in my mind.

I swallowed hard. Now was not a good time for this conversation, and to be honest, I just didn't want to admit that I was wrong this whole time, that while I was judging him for being a demon I wasn't even human myself.

'Nothing I want to share with you right now, Luka.' My tone was firm and the hurt that crossed his face was like a punch to the gut.

His teeth clenched, jaw muscles flexing as he stepped forward, extending his hand to my wrist without a word.

I gave it to him and his eyes flared yellow as he pulled my wrist to his mouth and sank his teeth into my skin. The pinch was painful for a second until the drug of his bite entered my veins and I felt a mellow calm overtake me. It would have been enjoyable if not for the death glare Luka was giving me. His nostrils flared, his eyes burned, and I was sure that he might actually hate me in that moment.

Whatever. He had a fiancée to lick his wounds, I couldn't be bothered to worry about hurting his feelings. He clearly wasn't worried about mine. With a jerk, he tore his teeth away and dropped my wrist like it was a hot stone. Turning his back, he stormed out of the apartment, leaving me feeling lost.

"That was awkward," Liv said behind me.

"That was like angry sex … without the sex," Sage offered.

"Alright, just a lovers' quarrel, let's move on. I'm driving." Demi shook some keys in her hand.

Lovers' quarrel without the love. What did that make it? Then it was just a fight. I realized then that I was more hurt by his engagement to Cassara than I realized. Even if it was out of his control, after that kiss … things had changed between us and I was still so gutted by the loss of Sterling and my entire old life that I'd actually been excited at the prospect of running back to Luka. Of having him to comfort me. Now that was gone and I was just bitter.

This was going to be a long month.

DEMI DROVE us in a brand new white Range Rover across the border from Vampire City into Werewolf City. It was fascinating to see the old Gothic cathedral buildings that the vampires preferred give way to glass and steel and modernity that the werewolves seemed to love. However, the land was marred with the signs of war. Scorched earth, tumbled buildings, half blown off trees. But there was still beauty here, and the rebuilding seemed to be in full effect. Tractors, cement trucks, and construction workers were seen at almost every intersection as we made our way through the downtown.

It looked so *normal*. Like Downtown Spokane but smaller. There was a hotel that looked like it had seen better days, a bookstore, coffee shop, clothing store. I knew Liv was thinking the same thing because of the surprise on her face.

"This is where the city wolves live." Demi gestured to lands around us. "But I'm half Paladin, those are the old-school magic wolves, and we live in the Wild Lands at the edge of the border."

Whoa.

There were two types of wolves? I didn't know that.

"That's where Marmal will be and where I will take you. If anyone knows about the breeding program, it's her."

I just nodded absentmindedly, taking it all in. A few moments later we'd pulled up to the gates of a school. *Sterling Hill* it read, and my heart pinched.

Sterling.

Liv reached out and grasped my hand, noticing the similarity in the name.

I hoped Maz would have reunited his head to his body and buried him properly, but somehow I doubted it, which just made my need for revenge grow stronger.

Demi waved at a guard who stood at the gate, and then drove deeper into campus through a parking lot.

The place was a total construction zone. It looked like it had been completely shelled out in the war and was now being rebuilt. New grass was going in, fresh brick being laid, signs hung. It was clear that whatever war the vampires and were-wolves had, it had its fair share of casualties. Now I knew why it was so important to get Luka crowned king. The werewolves couldn't take another hit while they were rebuilding.

Pulling into a parking spot in front of some electric scooters, Demi threw the car in park and stepped out. "No cars can go to Paladin Village," she said.

Liv and I shared a look.

Interesting.

Demi hopped on a scooter and waved for us to follow as she took off down a pathway.

"I haven't ridden a scooter since I was twelve," Liv whispered to me.

I grinned. "Ride on back. I'll drive us."

I jumped on a scooter and Liv stepped behind me, holding loosely onto my waist as I flipped the green switch and took off down the path after Sage and Demi.

Liv let out a whoop of excitement and I grinned.

Sage's red hair was flying like a flag in the wind and she looked back at me grinning. "Woo hoo!" she yelled, going faster and cutting right, down a path that led into the thick forest.

We zipped our scooters through the trees onto a freshly paved roadway. Like Demi said, it wasn't big enough for a car, but it was the perfect size for our little two-wheeled scooters. Sunlight pierced the canopy of trees as we passed and I inhaled, taking in the scents of the forest. Dew, pine, earth. A peacefulness came over me and I sighed in relief. There was something special about these woods. The trees thinned up ahead and opened into a clearing.

Demi slowed. She pulled her bike into a little parking lot off to the side that looked to be made specially for them and dismounted. After Sage parked hers, we did the same and jumped off.

I peered over Demi's shoulder and surveyed the land.

It was … beautiful. Untouched by the technology of the city we just left. Little brick buildings and quaint cobblestone walkways dotted the village. Flowers and veggies gardens were tended with care as people milled about on foot. It was like I'd been brought back in time. Something about this place immediately felt special.

A man approached us. He was shirtless, looked to be chiseled from rock, and had a long scar across his face. His brown skin shone in the sunlight.

"Alpha." He bowed.

"Yum," Liv whispered.

"Married unfortunately, and kinda a dick sometimes," Sage added.

Demi grinned at our conversation. "Rab, these are my friends, Aspen and Liv. We're here to see Marmal."

He nodded. "She's in the barn with Pearl."

With that, Demi started to walk through the town and we followed. Rab eyed us suspiciously as we walked by him, but he said nothing. We passed people coming in from the fields carrying baskets of corn and squash. A few wolves prowled the road, their noses to the ground. Liv and I shared a wild-eyed look. Werewolves or just real wolves? It was hard to tell. They looked small, but either way it was a bit unsettling.

Demi followed my gaze. "Werewolf pups. Learning to scent for hunting."

Those were werewolf *children?*

I was so spellbound by the village that I didn't realize we had reached the barn Rab had spoken of. Giant and red, it loomed over the tall trees. A creek ran behind it in the distance.

"Oh!" Demi spun, wide-eyed. "I forgot to warn you. Pearl is a dragon. So yeah ... prepare for that."

I could feel my eyelids open wider with each word she spoke, and my neck craned in order to hear her better.

"I'm sorry. Dragon?" Liv stepped forward as my mouth went dry.

Demi nodded, grinning. "Friendly dragon."

Sage bobbed her head up and down. "*Badass* friendly dragon."

I couldn't tell if they were messing with us or not.

Dragon, I mouthed to Liv, who just shrugged.

Had to be a practical joke. Dragons weren't a thing.

But no one was laughing…

Demi reached out and pulled the handle of the barn door wide. I stayed where I was, unsure if I was ready to actually see a dragon.

An animalistic chuffing noise came from inside as Demi called out to her friend Marmal in greeting, and Liv and I both glanced at each other nervously. Reaching out, Liv grabbed my hand and yanked me forward, pulling us both inside.

Holy crap.

My gaze skipped right over the troll girl with tiny tusks poking out of her cheeks and went right to the freaking white dragon!

She was … huge … and … real. I froze, unmoving, unbreathing as my gaze ran over her pearlescent scales. She stood over twenty feet tall and bent her head down to nuzzle the troll girl, who I assumed was Marmal, as she stroked her neck. There were horns on the top of her head and the back of her tail, which I could see would be useful in battle.

"Hey, Marmal, this is Aspen and Liv." Demi gestured to us both. "And they've clearly never seen a dragon."

Demi and Sage both laughed as Liv and I closed our open mouths and shook ourselves from our stupor.

"Sorry. It's nice to meet you." I giggled nervously and faced the girl, really taking her in. I'd seen pictures of the troll people but never one in person. She had long brown hair tied into a braid at her back. The tusks that stuck out of her cheeks were tiny compared to the male trolls I'd seen in photos, and there was something beautiful about her that I couldn't explain. She smiled at me kindly and placed a fist over her chest. "Well met, Aspen."

I just nodded, unsure what the customs of her people were.

"Hey." Liv waved awkwardly, and Marmal gave her the same greeting, fist over chest.

"So, we need your help, Marmal." Demi held out her hand in my direction. "Papers," she whispered to me.

Right. I was still shocked at the freaking dragon!

I reached into my pocket and unfolded the papers about our *breeders*. I'd left the note from Sterling behind. That felt too private to share with a complete stranger.

Demi handed it to the girl and I wondered how some troll woman would know anything about this —until she started to read it and the color drained from her face.

"Did you see anything like this in your year with the fey? It reminds me of the stuff Trip did with Pearl," Demi added.

I wondered what her year with the fey entailed and what had happened to Pearl, and who Trip was, but kept my mouth shut.

Marmal looked over at me and Liv, her eyes clouding with darkness. "This is about you? These are your names?" There was compassion in her voice, and I nodded.

"We thought we were fully human until a few days ago." I could feel my cheeks redden. It still felt weird to say that.

Marmal sighed, handing the paper back to Demi, and looked me right in the eyes. "There is a baby farm deep in Dark Fey Territory. I haven't seen it, but I heard about it during my time there. I could probably find it based on the description of the mountains and waterways."

"BABY FARM?" Liv screeched, saying what I was thinking.

Marmal nodded. "That's what they called it. A human woman traveled through the barn I worked at to buy some of them. She had a few Ithaki companions with her."

Bile rose in my throat and I suddenly felt sick. A whimper ripped from Liv's mouth and I reached out and grasped her hand.

We were both thinking the same thing: Who was the human woman Marmal had met?

"What did she look like? The human woman?" I asked.

Demi and Sage lowered their heads as if in reverence. They must have sensed the shock this news brought us.

"She was dressed oddly. In a robe and hair covering. Older woman, maybe in her late fifties or sixties."

Maz.

Instead of the unbridled rage I expected, a deep sadness bloomed in my heart. Even after all of the evidence against her, I had hoped it was a mistake and that somehow my mentor was innocent. It felt like the death of a mother and grandmother all at once.

"Can you take us to this place? We could do a scouting trip and be back in time for dinner?" Demi said.

Today!

"Ohh yes. Can Pearl fly us?" Sage asked. "I miss

adventure. I'm bored being Walsh's little puppy and following him all over the place." A pout pulled at her lips.

"Take us there! Right now?" Liv gasped.

On a dragon no less. I grinned. It did sound kind of exciting, and as long as I was back in time for anything Luka needed, I wasn't exactly abandoning him.

"Can you? Please?" I stepped forward, hoping to show this girl I barely knew how much it would mean to me.

She sighed, looking back at Pearl. The dragon looked into the girl's eyes and something passed between them. Could they communicate?

"Alright, a quick trip to look. But that's it. We're not starting any more wars," Marmal added.

Demi gave her a lopsided grin. "That, we agree on."

***

RIDING on a dragon was exactly what I thought it would be. Thrilling, terrifying, and kind of freaking cool. Pearl had these tiny horns you could hold on to, and we sat behind her one after the other like we were all riding a giant motorcycle.

"Girl power!" Sage thrust her fist into the air as we flew over the Troll Village lands.

We all laughed and held on tightly, looking around in wonder. Marmal took the time to point out some farm fields and burned-down crops, explaining it used to be her family farm. Demi reached out and squeezed her shoulder in comfort. There was a sadness in Marmal's voice, but I didn't ask how it burned down. Only nodded in understanding. Everyone had a story and everyone was fighting an internal battle that most knew nothing about. We flew for over a half hour looking down at the troll villagers. It was cool to see them tilling the fields and exchanging at the market.

They looked like a peaceful people. Much like the Paladins, they seemed to live off the land without any technology or modern conveniences.

Marmal had explained that Pearl had some kind of cloaking magic. I didn't really understand how it worked, but there was a visible sheen to the air around us, like a bubble we were trapped inside. Pearl swooped low to the ground, passing a few fey as we crossed the border, and they didn't look up at us, so clearly it masked us from sight.

'Where are you?' Luka's voice suddenly blared in my head. *'I had some free time so I thought I would come visit Sawyer and he says he hasn't seen you.'*

Crap.

'I'm with Demi.' Less information was best right now.

'Where, Aspen? We checked the Paladin lands. Where exactly are you?' The possessiveness in his voice pissed me off.

'Why? Afraid I'll die and you'll starve?'

He growled in my head. *'Aspen...'*

Whatever, might as well tell the truth, he was going to find out anyway. *'I'm currently flying on a dragon over the Fey Lands.'* I dropped the truth bomb and felt him recoil emotionally as shock ran through our bond.

'You're what!?' he roared so loud I winced.

'We're on a little scouting mission, nothing dangerous, I promise not to die.'

Hurt colored our connection, seeping from him and then into me. *'Aspen, what are you hiding from me? What don't you trust me with?'*

The way he said it gutted me. It wasn't that I didn't trust him, it was that I was scared and mad and a little embarrassed about the way I'd treated him when we first met, when I was no perfect Godly specimen myself.

'I do trust you, Luka.' My heart softened. *'It's... personal ... and really bad. Earth shattering actually.'* I hadn't even told him that Sterling died. Shoving

things in my deal-with-later pile was working, but for how long?

'Bad. Earth shattering? Shit, Aspen, tell me. Now I'm worried.'

"It's down there!" Demi whisper-screamed over the wind, pointing to a small village that was surrounded by a tall fence that was tipped with barbed wire.

'I'll tell you tonight. Promise. Gotta go now.' I hoped Luka wouldn't be too pissed, but by the scream of frustration he left on his departing out of my head, I wasn't sure I would get my wish.

"It's like a jail," Liv observed.

I leaned over the side of Pearl and looked down as she circled the top of the village. It was smaller than I imagined. I counted eight little huts with thatched roofs and a larger barn type building in the center of the encampment. The tall walls rose up around the structures, looming and casting a shadow over everything.

There was a well at the back wall, and I watched as a woman pulled a bucket of water up with skinny arms. Another woman, in her early twenties and fully pregnant, waddled across the yard with a child on her hip. The kid looked about three years old. My eyes scanned rapidly, noting that of the dozen or more women I saw, nearly every single one was pregnant and nearly every one had a child with them of varying ages. From a toddler to a teen.

"Why keep the children? I thought they sold them?" Sage asked, as confused as I was.

I peered closer and noticed the women's feet were bound, two cuffs held by a chain between to keep them from running.

Anger built inside of my chest so tightly it felt like a bomb ready to explode.

"I don't know," Demi growled. "But we are getting every single one of them out of there. Now. Let's land and fight." Demi slipped off her cuffs and my eyes widened.

I didn't bring any weapons, thinking this only a scouting mission, but already I was eyeing things on the ground I could use. A sharpened stick, an axe. Demi was right to be enraged, these women and children were clearly being mistreated and we could easily take them out of here now. I noticed no guards, which was surprising considering how well protected the fence was, and the chains on the women. Clearly they were valuable to someone.

"Hell yes," Liv growled, making a fist as she glared at the neglected women down below. If our mothers were down there … I couldn't even fathom that.

Marmal pulled a shotgun from beneath her cloak and grinned.

"Okay, this is happening." I rolled my neck out, prepared for the surprise raid. The women couldn't see us yet, but as Pearl descended they became clearer. Dirt-stained cheeks, sun-kissed skin, scratches and cuts on their legs and arms.

When we were just ten feet from the ground, I saw her: a woman of Asian descent with long black hair who looked to be in her early forties. I always wondered which parent I'd gotten my Asian heritage from, and without the bleaching and bottle dying, my hair was black as ink.

Mom?

She walked with a teenager who looked like a miniature version of her, and it felt like I'd been punched in the gut. A sister?

"The kids are the next breeders. They keep one to keep it all going," I said aloud as it hit me.

That was my mother and that was my sister. A future breeder.

Bile rose in my throat at the thought of the sweet teenager before me becoming a—

Pearl shrieked and a zapping sound cracked throughout the space. A bubble-like rainbow of magic appeared over the encampment, as if it were topped in a protective dome. Everyone below looked up.

Pearl shot into the sky as our own protective shield dropped, and for a split second the Asian woman looked up at me. We locked eyes and her hand went to her throat in shock. Pearl frantically flew higher just as a dozen figures in black cloaks appeared out of nowhere. When I say nowhere, I mean one second they weren't there and the next they were. Like they themselves had been cloaked as well and now that cloak fell away.

"Munai!" Demi shouted just as one of the cloaked figures stepped forward and pulled back their hood, looking up into the sky.

Holy demon from hell.

My blood ran cold as I gazed upon the creature before me. I couldn't believe I'd spent my entire life thinking vampires were evil. No, this monster was the epitome of evil. It wasn't the long stringy dark hair or the black, claw tipped fingers that frightened me. I could even get past the black network of veins running up its face. It was the eyes that made my stomach go sour.

All black. No white or color in them.

Dear God, protect us. I sent up a silent prayer just as the creature opened its mouth and screamed. A black blob flew from its throat and opened like a net, coming right for us.

What the heck!?

"Retreat!" Demi cried as Pearl tried to veer out of the way. The net grew wider as it approached us, as if it were sensing how big Pearl was and adjusting its size. I peered closer and noticed it moved like a shimmer of black oil, restless and *alive.*

Liv and I started to recite the *Hunter's Prayer* just as Sage stood and leapt off of the dragon with a battle cry. Her arm was extended, and in it, a giant sword.

"Can she fly?" I screeched, panic gripping me. Maybe she had powers I didn't know about yet.

"Nope," Demi growled as Pearl dropped suddenly.

I clenched my thighs to keep from being thrown off the beast. Darting my gaze around, I followed Sage's descent as she collided with the black, oily net, right before it could reach us. It wrapped around her like an octopus, tightening and slithering.

We sank like a stone. Pearl threw herself under Sage while the feisty redhead hacked at the black net with her sword like a madwoman, cutting shreds into it.

I was simultaneously horrified and in awe of her

brave act. But I had no time to dwell on it, because she was going to be on top of us in moments.

Demi thrust her arms out and a shockwave burst from her palms, slamming into Sage and slowing her descent. Peering up as she fell, I readied myself. She was headed right for me.

"Get my legs!" I cried to Liv, and stood up on the dragon's back, just as Sage fell like a ton of bricks into my arms. I swayed backward, but Liv gripped my ankles hard, planting me firmly to the spot. Some of the black netting was still on Sage's body, one large piece twisted around her arm, cutting into the skin. But the majority of it had fallen to the ground, bypassing Pearl.

With Liv's help, I crouched into a sitting position just as Sage wailed in pain in my arms. The moment my butt hit Pearl, I was free to help wrestle the black netting off of her arm. I grasped it and it coiled tighter like a snake. It was *alive*.

Demi was shouting directions at Marmal and Pearl. The dragon pumped her wings, taking us high above the barrier of the village.

Liv slipped a knife into my hand and I sawed at the net, careful not to cut Sage. Finally, it fell away like black noodles.

Sage panted, draped across Pearl as she looked up at the sky.

"You are crazy!" Demi scolded her.

"I knew if that net got around Pearl's wings we were *all* going down," Sage argued as I helped her sit up. Red welts marred her skin where the net had touched her.

Demi growled low in her throat and her eyes went yellow. "Okay, smart, but crazy. Don't do that again."

I peered at the village, now fading away into the distance and at the women who gathered, looking up into the sky in desperation.

What had started as a simple spying mission had nearly become our deaths.

"Who were those demons?" I growled, thinking of the creature who'd spewed the black netting.

Demi whistled low, readjusting the cuffs on her wrists. "Darkest, most evil fey you ever met. High priestess fey. Power like no other. Munai."

"I counted six of them," Liv added, and Demi nodded.

"And there could be more inside," Sage offered.

We were all thinking it, but no one had said it yet, so I guessed I would be the first one.

"We're going back to save them, right? We can't let them stay there like that," I said.

Demi just nodded once and then set her jaw in grim determination.

Liv leaned into me, her lips pulling her beautiful face into a frown. "Aspen … I think that lady was your mom. She looked just like you."

Hearing her say out loud what I'd been thinking made tears prick the edges of my eyes.

Mom.

Mother.

I couldn't even fathom it. And that girl with her … would she be my sister? It was too much.

"We have to go back," I croaked, as Pearl flapped her wings hard through the air and we headed back to Paladin lands.

"Oh, we're going back with backup, and that entire place will burn," Demi confirmed.

She was an alpha, so I didn't take her declaration lightly. She had power, and I clung to her promise tightly as we flew back to the Paladin village.

"I CAME AS SOON as I could, what's going on?" Luka looked so sexy in his black button-down shirt and dark wash jeans. His hair was gelled back in a swoop. I was momentarily speechless, just gazing at him. Then I remembered why I'd called him out here to the Paladin lands. Demi and Sawyer were waiting for us in the meeting hall, which also looked a lot like a church to me. It was nearly nighttime and I needed to bring Luka inside to talk about what we'd just seen and the strategy for saving the women, but I wanted to tell him about everything first.

I suddenly felt like I was going to be sick. Telling him I wasn't human felt almost too big.

"Sterling found something and called me the day that I ran out," I started.

Luka nodded. "I remember you didn't want me to go with you." There was a slight anger in his tone.

"When I got to the park, there was a box with Sterling's head in it." Luka gasped and my throat tightened. Before I knew what was happening, he'd pulled me into his arms. He was so fast, I didn't even see him move, I was just suddenly enveloped in the pressure of his touch, his smell, him. A sob tried to escape me but I swallowed it down, which caused a strangled whimper to leave my throat, and Luka just held me tighter. He knew Sterling was my ex; he knew what he had meant to me.

"Shit, Aspen, I didn't know. Why didn't you tell me?" He released me and stared at my face as if looking for evidence that I was okay or on the verge of a mental breakdown.

I swallowed hard. "Cassara." The one word was all it took for him to freeze up. Shame burned his cheeks and he nodded.

"You were trying to show me papers and she interrupted you." He rubbed his forehead as if in pain at the memory. "Aspen, what was on the papers? Was it about Sterling?"

That was a good lead-in for my next bomb drop. I handed him the papers.

"Luka … I'm not human. None of the hunters are. Sterling found this out and died to get me this information."

His eyes widened as they read over the papers.

He actually swayed as if a strong wind might knock him over. "I thought I tasted … but it was too faint," he said to himself. "Aspen … you're Ithaki?"

I nodded, unsure what that word really meant other than fey mutt.

Luka plopped down, right there on the brick steps to the meeting hall, and stared at the papers.

"You're not fully human," he mused.

Wow. I wasn't really prepared for *his* shock. I thought his first instinct would be to try to get me back for all the times I'd called him a monster.

I sat down next to him. "I'm not. And the 'breeder' who is my mother is being held in a heavily guarded colony in the dark fey lands. We went and saw her today."

His head snapped up. "That's where you went? *Dark* Fey Territory!"

I shrugged. "It was totally safe."

Luka wouldn't stop staring at the papers so I yanked them from his hand. "Yes I'm part fey. Let's move on to where we rescue the women being held against their will. We will need an army, a vampire army," I urged him.

He looked over at me, going very still. "Aspen, I want to, I do, but—"

I stood suddenly, crossing my arms. "Don't you dare say no."

He stood too, reaching out to grasp my upper arms, and then trailed his fingers down them, sending chills along my spine. "Aspen, if anyone you care about is trapped somewhere, I will stop at nothing to free them, but I'm not king yet and I'm still a wanted felon. I don't have an army to offer now like I will have in a few weeks."

My heart fell. In a few weeks they could be dead or moved. Now that we'd seen them, the Munai might just take them all to another safe house.

The door opened and Sage peeked her head out. "Ya'll better get in here and talk some sense before they get divorced over this."

Loud voices filtered outside and we stood, stepping into the space. I was right, it was a church of sorts. Pews sat in neat rows, and Sawyer and Demi were sitting across from two of them, facing each other. Sawyer bounced an adorable baby on his knee as the little boy chewed on his fingers.

"Demi, my love, we just got out of a war," Sawyer warned his wife.

She growled low in her throat. "I know that, I'm the one who helped us win it!"

Burn.

Sawyer's eyebrows bunched together. "What would you have me do? Pull my men off rebuilding the city to go traipsing through Dark Fey Territory and start a war with them?"

Demi stood and glared down her husband, her eyes flashing yellow. "Fine. I'll go with the Paladins. We can handle it alone."

She turned to walk away and Sawyer groaned. "Get back here, woman! Of course I'll fight with you. Geeze."

Demi froze and turned, noticing Luka and I for the first time. Winking at me, Demi then faced Luka. "Are you in or will you break a nail, *Prince*?"

Luka looked at Sawyer: "What are the rules about me backtalking your wife?"

Sawyer chuckled. "Don't do it."

Demi walked over to Luka with a grin. "Seriously though, this could unite our people. If you brought in the vamps, and we brought the wolves, then together we can save the slaves from this human-fey baby farm."

Luka visibly winced at the word *slaves*, and then winced again at *baby farm*. "Like I just told Aspen, I don't have an army yet. I'm not king. I'm still a felon wanted by the Magical Creature Council but—"

"Did someone say 'felon,'" a familiar voice called out from behind me, and we all spun.

Walsh was standing in the open doorway with Bennet and one other male I didn't know, but it had to be Talon, the final member of their little prison *Five Crew* that Luka had told me about.

Sawyer burst up from where he sat and handed Demi the baby. Both he and Luka stalked over to the three guys and pulled them into a group bro hug.

"They're adorable," Liv said beside me.

"I want to get them all matching custom t-shirts," Demi said, bopping the baby on her hip.

"It will say 'Hot felons,'" Sage added, and we all burst out laughing at the mental image of them wearing such a thing.

"Why are you here?" Sawyer asked them.

"Walsh told us you needed help with breaking free some prisoners." Bennet gestured to Walsh, who looked to Sage and winked. Sage visibly swooned, her eyes going all goo-goo gaga and I was suddenly insanely jealous of all these solid relationships around me. All I ever wanted from Sterling was commitment. House, kids, ring. I was that chick. Instead, I fell for a walking dead guy who was engaged to a walking dead girl.

Cue mental breakdown.

I corrected the use of his word prisoner: "Slaves—breeding slaves."

Bennett looked to Demi. "You say the Munai are guarding the camp?"

She nodded once. "At least half a dozen."

Bennet let out a low whistle. He was the resident fey of the group, so he probably knew the most about the Munai.

"We aren't going to be able to take on half a dozen Munai with brute force. We'll need witches too."

Witches. My blood ran cold. I'd never met a witch … that I knew of. They could be anywhere though. They were the most likely to be able to blend in with the humans.

"Won't be a problem. I can get at least five of them," Demi added.

My heart swelled with pride as this woman who I barely knew so easily leant her forces to a cause that didn't affect her in any way. I wanted to tell them that they didn't have to do this, but I refrained because I really wanted them to. I *needed* them to. Liv and I couldn't do this alone.

"If we can prove the dark fey are keeping Ithaki against their will, we could use it in a war crimes case to absolve us of our treason," Sawyer added.

"Treason." My mouth opened in shock.

Sawyer nodded, looking at Demi. "If we go marching into fey territory without permission and blow up their buildings and kill their Munai, we will have a lot to answer for."

Yikes. When he put it that way, it sounded bad.

"The Magical Creature Council will come sniffing around," Walsh added.

Everyone looked to Luka then, who simply nodded. "My first act as king will be to pardon us all, and I will be exempt from trial based on diplomatic immunity."

Whoa. The plan was shaping up even better than I thought.

"Then we need to wait until you become king or we all get locked up in Magic City Prison," Sage offered. "And that doesn't work well for my fall wedding plans."

Walsh gave a little chuckle.

Demi said what I was thinking: "If we don't act quickly, they'll move them, I know it."

I nodded. "Then they might be forever lost to us."

"But if we act too quickly, we may win and get locked up," Sawyer told his wife.

I chewed on my lip, trying to think of a solution. Now more than ever before, I needed Luka to become king. With the vampire forces at our disposal and his pardoning power, we could totally pull this off.

"We wait," Luka declared, one hand stroking his chin. "The second I'm crowned king, we storm the Fey Lands and free all of the women and children. Until then, we assign an elite group of spies to watch the camp and make sure that if the women are moved, we know the new location. Let them get comfortable somewhere else thinking they have successfully hidden, then we come for them in the dead of night."

Chills rose up my arms at his declaration. I'd never been more attracted to him than I was in this moment. My heart hammered in my chest and his eyes met mine.

Walsh smirked. "Elite spy group?"

Luka chuckled. "You, Talon, and Bennett. Sawyer and I need to stay visible."

The three of them nodded and it was decided.

We wait…

As hard as that was, I could wait a few weeks if it meant I knew we had a greater success of getting my mom and the others out.

With that, we disbanded and Liv, Demi, Sage, and I headed back to the guest cottage. But all the while my mind raced with flashes of her face. *My mom.* I just hoped she survived long enough for me to meet her in person properly.

NEXT MORNING, I awoke feeling different. My entire life I'd always had a bit of a hole inside myself. Growing up without a mother and father will do that. I was never really adopted; Maz was just our mentor and leader—and sometimes mother figure, but not the one that tucks you in bed and sings you songs every night. I never had that, and now that I'd gotten a glimpse of my mother, I wanted it. After showering, I dressed and shuffled into the hallway to find Gunner standing in the kitchen wearing an apron and cooking eggs and bacon.

"Good morning, Miss Rose. I hope it's okay that I let myself in. Luka has requested that I provide adequate nutrition for you and the other feeders. He's asked that I serve you breakfast and bring you to the banquet hall."

Feeder. I would never get used to that word.

I swallowed hard. "Banquet hall?"

He plopped a spoonful of eggs, two pieces of bacon, and a piece of toast onto a plate and then handed me a glass of orange juice.

"That's where today's battle is, the fight got moved up." He nodded, his shiny-bald head reflecting the overhead kitchen lights. I stared at his pointy ears, getting distracted as I reached up to touch my own. They were slightly pointier than a human's, but … I'd never really thought about it until now.

"So Luka will battle every day until he's the last one standing?" I tore off a hunk of bacon and chewed and Gunner watched me closely. I was slightly more invested in Luka becoming king now.

"Not every day. Some days are physical battle days, in which he will need a feeder on call like today, and others are mental exercises, war games, propriety testing."

Propriety testing? I scrunched up my face. "That sounds horribly boring." I went to put another bite of eggs to my mouth and Gunner watched me raise the spoon like a hawk. Dropping the fork to my plate, I pinned him with a glare.

"Either you've poisoned this or Luka has tasked you with making sure I eat all of my food like a five-year-old. Which is it?" I growled.

His cheeks turned rosy. "Sorry, ma'am. No poison. It's the latter. Luka said you might be … feisty, but that I should be sure you eat properly to sustain good health during the feedings."

I groaned, ripping off a bite of toast and chewing it aggressively. Dammit, I wasn't sure if that was annoying or romantic!

I changed the subject. "So you're fey?"

He shook his head. "Ithaki. Fey-vampire mix." He peeled his lips back to show tiny vampire canine teeth.

I froze, totally weirded out by the fact that the fey could mix with any of the races. Hearing it from Luka was one thing, seeing it was another.

"Ithaki?" I tried to play dumb. I'd heard a bit about them at the society, and from what Demi told me yesterday, which was a whole lot of nothing. I wanted to know more.

He nodded. "Fey have special magic that assists with the interbreeding of their DNA with any of the other races."

Crazy.

"Even humans?" I tried to act casual but he froze, looking at me more minutely.

"It's forbidden of course, to mix magical races and humans, but I suppose it would work."

"Cool," I said, then changed the subject quickly. "So who do you want to be king?"

He relaxed, his shoulders softening as he cleared away the dishes. "Makes no matter to me. I get paid either way, but Master Luka seems like he would be the most tolerable."

I bobbed my head in agreement. "Who is the least tolerable?" I wanted to know who Luka was up against. I knew the entire family tree.

His features sharpened, and he eyed me with suspicion. Probably thought I was trying to get him into trouble.

"Is Morgana one of the contestants?" I amended.

He relaxed a little at that and nodded. "She is."

Great. The aunt who paid the Shadow Bloods to kill him that night at Bang.

When I put the last piece of bacon in my mouth, he stopped watching me so closely.

I showed him my empty plate. "You can report to Prince Luka that I have finished my breakfast like a good little girl."

He chortled. "Yes, ma'am. Why don't you change and then I will bring you to the banquet hall." He indicated to a stack of clothes that were folded on the chair next to me. I picked them up, expecting it to be a uniform of sorts, and frowned when I saw just an oversized t-shirt and sweatpants.

"Uhh, why?" I looked down at my skinny ripped jeans and midriff camisole.

When I looked up at Gunner, his cheeks were pink. "Miss Bane wanted me to impress upon you that she's taken note of your ... beauty, and if you wish to remain as Luka's feeder, you must try to ... dress down in his presence."

My mouth popped open. Dress down! In this potato sack? Cassara, that controlling little witch. I stood up and glared at Gunner. "You're right. I should change. I'll be ready to go in a minute."

Grabbing the clothes Cassara had sent for me, I stormed back to my room. The second I got inside, I chucked them against the back wall and opened my duffle bag, because I had yet to fully unpack.

If Cassara wanted to play, I could play.

GUNNER DIDN'T SAY a word when I walked out of the room in my new outfit. He just shook his head in resignation. Now I walked up to the banquet hall with Gunner wearing tiny jean shorts and black fishnet stockings, teamed with an emerald-green silk tank that had black lace trim. I'd also thrown on some smoky eye shadow and red lipstick to match my hair. All complete with my black leather knee-high boots.

Bring it, Cassara. You want me to look like a frumpy old feeder? Hah. Not while I was still breathing.

Stepping into the two open double doors, I was immediately brought into an inner hallway that led to another set of double doors. Outside those were two beefed-up vamp security guards. My hand absently went for my silver stake only to remember it wasn't there.

Some vampires can be friends, I reminded myself.

Gunner bowed slightly to the guards. "Miss Aspen Rose, feeder to Luka Drake."

One guard held out his hand and Gunner produced some paper that had an official looking seal. He inhaled as if smelling for my humanness, and I suddenly wondered if Luka had ever smelled the fourteen percent fey on me.

The guard's eyes ran down my body in a way that was *not* respectful and I instantly wanted to throat punch him.

The security dude nodded and opened one of the double doors.

Gunner bowed to me. "I'll have lunch ready when you get home."

He reminded me a lot of Kenzley and how he

always cared for us and made sure we were fed. I never had a dad but Kenzley was the closest thing to a father figure I would ever have. It made me sad that I would never see him again.

"Thank you, Gunner."

He backed away and the security guard gestured for me to step inside. "You may join the other feeders." He pointed to a corner of the room.

Feeder sounded dirty in his mouth, like he was saying the word *whore*.

I quickly stepped away from him and waltzed into the room, taking stock of my surroundings.

The far most right corner he had pointed to was really just a space with collapsible chairs. Eight of them. A mixture of human male and female feeders sat there. Some were reading, one was knitting, and a few were talking.

My gaze swiveled to the left, where grand bleachers were set up in ascending height.

Holy mother of Drakes.

My head nearly exploded as I scanned the faces of the people present. Keres, Georgio, Morgana, Isabella, Theo, Vera, Nico, all the bigwigs were here and all sitting as far apart from each other as possible. Each one had a significant other on their arm, and when my gaze landed on Cassara, I realized she was watching me, her eyes piercing right through me with hatred.

I smiled and gave her a little wave.

Luka hadn't seen me yet, but must have felt Cassara go rigid beside him. She leaned in and whispered something into his ear and he turned to look at me.

Good God, he was so good looking it actually hurt to stare at him. The moment our eyes met, his flared a hungry honey-yellow. He was shirtless, surprise, and his fists were wrapped in strips of cloth like a boxer ready for a match. Low slung basketball shorts hung off his hips, showcasing all of the taut yumminess. The wound from the other night was gone, hidden within the myriad of tattoos and scars across his abdomen.

The way he looked at me then made me feel like I was the only woman in the room. My heart thumped so loudly in my chest I was sure every single person could hear it.

Thump. Thump. Thump.

Luka Drake had this effect on me, an effect I'd tried to hide before, one I was in denial of, ashamed of. My mouth went dry as he raked his gaze slowly down my body, his dark hair pulled like a messy mop in front of his eyes.

I wanted him in the worst way possible.

'Are you trying to kill me?' he huffed into my mind. *'If I had a beating heart, it would stop right now.'*

I grinned, holding his gaze, delighted that my outfit had this effect on him.

'But seriously, Aspen, you need to play it safe or Cassara will erase you.' There was concern in his voice and it soured my mood.

I glared at her as she glared back, unaware I could speak into Luka's mind. *'Let her try.'*

I was a vampire hunter! Did he not realize that? I could take that witch down any day.

He shook his head sadly. *'It won't be her. It will be her security team, or she'll force me to remove you as my feeder. Please, Aspen. Next time, try not to be so damn...'*

He looked at a loss for words. *'Sexy,'* he finally said, sounding resigned.

He called me sexy. That was a win in my book, and Cassara had seen my direct refusal to wear her potato sack, so I was happy.

'Fine,' I growled. *'Next time I'll dress like a potato.'* I pouted, sticking out my bottom lip.

Even from here, I could see his gaze dropped to my lip and his eyes flared like burning embers in a dying fire.

Realizing what I'd done, I sucked my lip back into my mouth and swallowed hard.

'Why don't you sit with the others and I'll come get you for a feeding before my fight?'

I nodded sheepishly, already hating being relegated to the feeder corner.

After finding my place among the living, I picked at my purple nail polish as a handful of men set up an elevated stage with a wrestling mat in the center of the room. They brought out stands with various weapons hanging from them. I spotted an axe, sword, stake, and even a barbed chain.

My stomach turned to dread. Was Luka going to have to kill his family? That was messed up.

There was a red velvet rope partitioning off the rest of the giant space. I wondered why until the double doors opened and hundreds of vampires started to trickle in.

This was going to be a spectacle, a public fight to the death.

How barbaric.

A beautiful female with strawberry blond hair started to set up a mic and PA system and I wished Liv was here for comfort.

What if Luka died? What if I had to sit here and watch him be killed? The thought was sickening, but it was not lost on me that just over a week ago I was trying to kill him myself. It was crazy how much a person could change in a week.

"Feeders, please report to the feeding room. Feeders to the feeding room," the female announcer said over the microphone.

Everyone around me stood and I fumbled, standing as well.

I had no idea where the feeding room was here. I followed the handful of feeders as a security guard led us out of the giant ballroom, down a hallway, and then inside of a large room. At the left and right wall were several doors, like phonebooths all with a name above them.

I scanned the sign that read *Luka Drake* and stepped toward it. One by one, all of the feeders disappeared into their respective booths, so I did the same. I stepped inside of the dark, barely-lit coffin. It was akin to a small utility closet with a single black-light hanging overhead. I barely had time to register Luka's form before me when he zoomed forward, taking my face into his hands and pulling my lips to his mouth.

A gasp ripped from my lungs as he pushed his tongue inside my mouth in a surprisingly passionate kiss. I moaned, opening my mouth wider and wrapping my arms around his lower back, pressing him closer to me.

'Georgio said he wanted to switch feeders with me because you looked so delicious and I nearly lost my

mind,' he huffed inside my head, his hands trailing down my spine. *'I don't ever want to share you with another man. Ever.'*

Need surged inside of me as I clung to him, stroking his tongue with mine. My skin felt like it was on fire, leaving a trail of burning goosebumps wherever he touched me. *'Then don't. Ditch Cassara and I'm yours,'* I promised. It was a crazy thing to say, a promise that held weight, but I wanted to keep it. I wanted him. I knew this now. There was no more denying it.

He pulled back from me, eyes wild in the black-light. His entire skin glowed, teeth included. "Aspen... I can't do th—"

"Royals to the fighting mat," the announcer said over the speaker.

I swallowed hard, unsure where I stood with Luka now, but I was pretty sure he was about to say he couldn't do that. Pain sliced into my heart, filleting it right in half.

Kill me now.

I raised my wrist to his mouth, my heart aching at the thought of him marrying her. I'd all but just proposed that he be with me instead and he'd rejected me.

I'm an idiot.

With a frown, he unceremoniously took my

wrist into his mouth and drank. Pleasure and pain rushed through me in equal measure. I'd just asked him to leave Cassara and be with me and he did nothing.

The silence ebbed between us, and with each second I stacked a wall around my heart. It was like Sterling all over again. When I cared, I cared too deeply, and I got burned. I was always the one throwing my feelings out there, abandoning caution and in the end getting hurt. I needed to put my focus on other things, I couldn't just be Luka's little beck-and-call girl. So while I was in Magic City I was just going to use my time here to help free my mom. I needed him to become king and keep his word on that.

When Luka pulled away from my wrist, he bent down and licked the last drop of blood off, continuing to stare at me. I felt guilt and anguish ebbing from him through our bond, but I ignored it.

"Aspen ... if you want to be with me, I could arrange a house to be built for you here. I could see you a few times a week, and after Cassara gave me two heirs I could leave her—"

I gasped, tearing my wrist from his hand. "Did you just ask me to be your mistress?"

How dare he!

"I ... I'm trying to find a way we can be together."

Shame burned in his voice as I stepped away from him.

"All royals, please report to the fighting mat," the announcer said, the command muffled in our tiny closet.

"I want you." Hurt crossed his face, still glowing from the blacklight as he reached for me. "More than I've ever wanted anything."

Tears lined my eyes, as my heart burned with the reality of our situation.

"You have to have children to be king? How is that even possible? You're a vampire and so is Cassara. You can't procreate."

He looked down at me sadly. "We grew up in a breeding farm similar to the one your mother is in. When I was seventeen, they … took sperm samples. The same with Cassara for her eggs. We have human embryos waiting to be inserted into a surrogate. Once the children come of age, they would be changed and the Drake line goes on forever."

I stumbled backward. "That's … you can't … how?" My mind spun with questions.

He was changed against his will?

"I would never do that to my children, but I need to get put into power before I can make changes," he pleaded with me.

A sob ripped from my throat at the sheer horror

of it all. He and Cassara already had embryos together?

"Luka Drake to the fighting mat!" The announcer sounded annoyed.

Luka nodded. "Now you see my entire life has been planned for me. I've had no say in any of this. I never wanted to be king until now. To save Walsh, Talon, Bennett, your mom. I'll do it for them."

Tears slid down my face and I nodded softly, coming to terms with our situation. Mistress or nothing. Those were my options.

"Good luck in your fight. I hope you win and get everything you want," I said sincerely, turning to leave the room. I wasn't going to waste my youth on another guy who couldn't commit to me. With each step I took away from Luka, I hardened my heart toward him. I wouldn't let him die of starvation, we would always have this bond and I would honor it, but I wasn't going to kiss him again, or flirt, or allow myself to be wooed by his charms. I wanted marriage, kids, and the whole package. Mistress wasn't enough.

6

THE FIRST FIGHT had already started, between Morgana and Keres, and I watched in horror as they tore each other apart. I didn't mind blood and gore, I was a hunter after all, but it seemed stupid to me that you would kill all of these royals just to have a last-man-standing type of thing. But the Drakes had bloodline in spades. There were over a hundred of them. Losing ten a year was nothing. And now that I knew about their little embryo breeding program, I was sickened by how long they could continue their line.

Forever?

The former mad king tore into Morgana but it was clear he was weakening. He swayed and then buckled under her. The female vampire stood with a feral grin, blood dripping from her dagger as she hovered over Keres, who lay on the floor.

He looked up at her, the oldest vampire alive, and didn't move.

"Do it," he begged, and I shifted uncomfortably in my seat. He was craving an end … that much was clear. Without so much as a pause for thought, Morgana slammed the dagger right into his heart and his body stilled, slowly drying up into a petrified husk and turning to ash.

Silence spread over the gathered crowd. There were hundreds of vampires present. They'd been cheering and screaming through the entire fight but now said nothing. There was no honor in killing someone who just lay there and asked for it.

"Morgana Drake. Winner!" the female announcer finally said and the crowd cheered, though it seemed forced. Morgana was bloody and beaten but still very much standing. With a nod she called her feeder over to her and the good-looking male human stood and approached her.

We were here to feed them so they could heal rapidly after a fight if injured; it was slightly horrifying. We were basically human coffee cups.

The female announcer looked down at a sheet she held in her hand and then pulled the microphone to her lips. "Next fight! Isabella Drake and Georgio Drake!"

Everyone fell into hushed silence. They were

brother and sister! My mouth hung open, horrified when I realized Keres, the mad king who'd just died, was their father. I couldn't imagine grieving my father and fighting my brother on the same day.

Izzy looked over at her brother and nodded once before standing. "I forfeit my right to the crown for all eternity," she stated, and the crowed rose up in murmurs, shouting and pointing her way.

Okay ... now that was interesting.

Morgana shot Izzy a scowl from her place on the mat where she had just finished feeding. "Coward!" she yelled up at Izzy.

Izzy flipped her the bird and then stepped down from the stands as security escorted her out.

Holy freaking crap!

I had no idea someone could forfeit their right to the crown and get out of the competition. I would do that too before I fought my own sibling. Izzy had just gained my respect in droves.

Everyone was silent, unsure what would happen next as Izzy was walked out the double doors.

The announcer looked perplexed, consulting her sheet of paper. "Okay! Isabella Drake has taken the coward's way out. That leaves us with…" She peered down at her paper again. "Georgio and Nico are the next fight!"

The crowd roared and my gaze flicked to Georgio.

The tall vampire looked to Luka and gave him a curt nod. He stood, and my stomach tied itself into a knot. Was he also going to—?

"I forfeit my right to the crown for all eternity," he said with a bit of a pained expression.

The entire crowd took a collective gasp, myself included.

Izzy hadn't just forfeited so that she wouldn't fight her own brother. Luka had formed allies and they were bowing to him left and right, that much was for sure. Pride swelled inside my chest. They believed he would be the best king and it brought tears to my eyes.

"Nonsense!" Morgana cried out as a huge grin spread across Luka's face. Cassara looped her arm through his and snuggled into him, glaring Morgana down. Well, at least she was sticking up for her man. I guess I should be grateful for that.

Theo stood. "It's clear some alliances have formed!" Theo was a badass vamp from what little I knew. He was Morgana's brother, but it was clear by the way he glared at his sister that they would have no problem tearing each other apart.

The announcer looked to the corner of the room, where a few old vampires sat. They reeked of power and wore long cloaks like they were born in another era altogether. I didn't notice them before, so they must have slid in while I was feeding Luka. "Alliances are not against the rules," one of them stated loudly for all to hear.

The announcer fumbled with her paperwork, clearly flustered. "Nico Drake and Luka Drake, you are next to fight—unless one of you wants to forfeit as well?" she growled as the crowd stayed silent.

I did a quick count of who was left. Morgana, Nico, Luka, Theo, and Vera. That was it. Five. Excitement thrummed through me. Maybe Luka could really be king and it would take less time than we thought, which meant saving my mom sooner.

"Oh, I'm fighting for *my* crown," Nico snapped and stood, pumping his hands into fists. Luka gave Nico a look of absolute hatred as Cassara placed a swift kiss on Luka's cheek, which knotted my stomach even more.

The crowd went wild, like they were a bunch of crazed maniacs who couldn't go without a fight. Morgana had left the mat and was now walking back up to her spot in the bleachers as Luka and Nico made their way to the mats. The crowd stomped their feet in anticipation and I couldn't help but feel sick at the way the vampires did this all so publicly.

'This is so messed up,' I told Luka.

He gave me a curt nod. *'And yet it's the most impor-tant part of the trials. No vampire will follow a leader who is weak.'*

That was a fair point.

'Use your compulsion!' I said suddenly, remem-bering he was a master of it.

'Against the rules. Besides, it has its consequences,' was all he said.

They both walked over to the weapons rack but Luka bypassed it, choosing nothing as Nico picked out the axe.

It felt like my eyes might fall out of my head. *'What are you doing? Grab a sword or something.'*

Luka looked over at me, then winked and my stomach dropped. Holy hell he was sexy. Maybe I should reconsider the mistress thing.

"Luka Drake is feeling brave and chooses no weapon!" the announcer stated.

The crowd went insane, screaming and beating on their chests in excitement.

God help them all. They were crazy.

I swallowed hard and the bell went off. The two men zoomed at each other and my heart leapt into my throat, where it would remain until Luka either won or died.

The two figures were almost too hard to track, but the second Nico stepped into Luka's space, he brought the axe down. Luka pulled his fist up and blocked the axe by grasping the handle and wrenching it out of Nico's hands.

The crowd nearly shook the walls with their cheering.

Luka chucked the axe to the side, grinning like a maniac.

Panic flickered across Nico's face, and then Luka turned into an absolute beast mode fighter. With his left leg, he swiped Nico off his feet, crashing him to the ground. Nico went backward and Luka took the advantage, sitting on Nico's stomach, pinning him. With no weapons, there was only one thing to do, and even though I had a strong stomach, I had to look away when Luka pummeled Nico's face with vampire speed and strength. The sound of breaking bones and gurgling filled the room and my stomach roiled.

There was some bad blood between these two. Luka was taking his time with him.

'Finish him!' I shouted as the crowd cheered.

"Luka is showcasing the skills he learned in Magic City Prison," the announcer said and everyone chuckled.

My gaze flicked to the older vamps, who looked absolutely overjoyed at the disgusting level of violence Luka was displaying.

Nico's face was pulverized; his hands started to twitch with each punch. The crowd grew silent but Luka kept punching, drenched in blood and gore.

'Luka. He's done. Kill him properly.' My heart seized me as I realized something was wrong. When I reached out to Luka, I felt a crazed and unbridled rage wash over me.

Luka slowed, seemingly realizing we were all watching him go psycho and no one was cheering anymore. Reaching out, he gripped the axe he'd tossed and held it to Nico's throat.

"*That* was for my sister." Luka spat in what used to be Nico's face, and brought the axe down on his neck.

I turned away, my heart pinching in my chest.

Sister? Luka had a sister? What the hell had Nico done to his sister? Confusion washed over me as Luka stood and Nico's body decomposed before us. Luka's chest shuddered as if he was trying to keep from crying. Vampires didn't breathe, so I knew he was struggling when I saw that.

"Luka Drake is the winner!" the announcer roared, and the crowd cheered wildly.

Luka blasted off the stage, passing me, and went out the double doors. Cassara stood, running after him and I wasn't sure what to do.

I wanted to go after him too.

"That's all we had scheduled for today. Final fights will be next week! We should have our king or queen crowned soon," the announcer purred into the microphone and everyone applauded.

A stone sank in my gut. I couldn't get Luka's monstrous rage out of my head. Not that I judged him for such a thing, but that kind of rage came from some serious pain, and if he was in pain I wanted to be with him.

That was for my sister.

Tears lined my eyes and I stood, slipping out the double doors and getting lost in the commotion of the crowd. One good thing about my bond with Luka was that if I focused on it and opened to it, I always knew where to find him.

I turned down the hallway and then came upon a door that said *Men's Locker Room* just as Cassara was leaving. I slipped into an alcove, hiding as she called out behind her. "Okay, see you at dinner then, babe!"

A crowd of vampires walked past and I bent, pretending to tie my shoe near the vase that was in the alcove as Cassara and the other vampires all went down the hall and out of sight.

I stepped up to the door and pushed it open a few inches, peering inside. No one in sight. The sound of rushing water filled my ears.

Mistress. The dirty word infiltrated my brain and

I considered it. I wanted Luka … bad. But I also wanted to save myself for my future husband. I wanted to be with a guy who wanted to be with me … publicly, and forever.

I opened myself to our bond, trying to see if he was better or still feeling raw after that fight. I wasn't prepared for the grief that slammed into my chest, nearly bringing me to my knees. Tears pricked my eyelids as I felt what Luka must be feeling.

Family.

Loss.

Sorrow.

Shame.

Regret.

Hatred.

It was all so strong it nearly consumed me. Stepping inside the locker room, I flicked the lock on the door behind me and padded over to the shower stall that had the curtain drawn. Without hesitation, I pulled the curtain back and stepped into the water to meet Luka face to face. His sharp intake of breath when he saw me was followed by a small whimper. I kept my eyes on his, not looking down at his nakedness no matter how much I wanted to. Not in this moment, not when he was so vulnerable.

"It hurts," he said, and I knew he didn't mean his hands or any physical injuries he had sustained. I nodded, tears streaming down my face as I grieved the loss of his sister whom I never knew. I sensed that she was younger and he loved her more than life itself. And she was gone and he couldn't protect her. That's all I knew, all I could pick up from the tornado of emotions slamming into me.

Reaching out, he pulled me into him and I pressed my face to his chest, water falling on my head and down my body, drenching us both. I wrapped my arms around his back and just held him while his chest heaved. We held each other for what felt like eternity, but must have only been a few minutes. Finally, the shuddering of his body slowed; the storm inside of him eased up the tiniest bit.

He pulled back, taking my face out of the water and stroking his thumb over my bottom lip, which sent a wave of fire through my body. "I want you, Aspen Rose, in every way possible. It *kills* me."

He ran his eyes slowly down my soaking wet form and heat burst to life between my legs. I wanted him too.

Rushing forward, I wrapped my arms around his neck and pulled his mouth to mine. A strangled moan ripped from his lips as I inserted my tongue into his mouth. The warm water trickled slowly down my neck and between our bodies.

His grief was like a raw open wound, and with

each kiss and lap of our tongues I felt it ease and stitch back together. He fumbled with the button of my shorts and I froze, pulling away from him to look at him more clearly. His fingers stopped just at the top of my underwear, his eyes like molten lava.

The only sound was water beating on tile and the panting of my breath, but now I was about to douse ice water on this fire.

"I'm a virgin," I blurted out.

The surprise on his face morphed into a satisfied grin. "That's the sexiest thing you've ever said."

Relief bloomed in my chest. You never knew where that sentence was going to go. It either freaked men out or they saw it as a mountain to conquer.

"Waiting for marriage, I assume?" he asked, fingers still stationed at the top of my underwear.

I nodded. I'd been raised my entire life by the hunter code, but even now that I knew it was distorted by Maz, I liked that I'd kept this special thing for myself and my future husband. Sex was sacred and I wanted to keep it that way.

His fingers inched downward and my head swam with dizziness as every inch of blood headed south-ward. "Is this okay?" he purred, leaning forward to nip my ear as I opened my legs and nodded.

His fingers crawled down my abdomen until they

rested on the most sensitive part of my body. My heart beat so frantically I could barely focus, the anticipation of what was coming nearly killing me. I leaned my pelvis into his hand; Luka trailed his tongue along my neck and a moan ripped from my throat.

"You are perfect, Aspen Rose. Absolutely perfect."

With his free arm, Luka scooped his hand under my butt and hauled me on top of him. I straddled my legs as he pinned my back against the tile wall, moving his thumb and finger expertly between my legs.

Warm water beat across his back as he trailed his teeth over my neck.

'Can I?' he asked.

I was on the edge of what would surely be a giant orgasm that would stop my heart and kill me. I wasn't sure how much more I could take before I shattered.

'Yes,' I growled, and his teeth sank into my skin.

Everything inside of me uncoiled in a millisecond and then exploded. My body rocked against his. I arched my back against the tile wall and cried out. Using my hands to grasp his biceps, I steadied myself as he drank from me, sending waves of pleasure not only throughout my body but into my soul.

In that moment, Luka and I became one, and a terrifying thought hit me.

I'm falling in love with him.

He was kind. Protective. Sexy. Powerful. Generous. All of the things I wanted in a man … sans heartbeat. He was the guy I'd been waiting for, a forever guy. Hell, he was even willing to get married and have kids, unlike Sterling.

Just not with me.

The waves of pleasure subsided and Luka pulled himself from my neck, and my shorts, and set me down, grinning.

He looked like he'd just won an award or something, and I was pretty damn sure if there was a trophy sitting around I would give it to him for his efforts.

I chuckled nervously. "So … that happened."

His smile slowly melted into a serious expression and he swallowed hard. "I can figure something out … maybe Cassara could give me heirs but I wouldn't have to marry her … I can look into the law—"

I reached out and placed a finger on his lips. "Cassara likes you. She will be loyal to you and you need to do the same. I won't be a side piece, Luka, and I need you to become king."

It was the most painful thing I'd ever said.

He looked terrified. "What are you saying?"

I swallowed hard. "This will never happen again." I gestured between us.

"No!" he growled, stepping closer to me as the water washed over him. "I've never wanted anything more than I want you."

I nodded, tears lining my eyes. "I believe that. But Walsh, and my mom, and everyone is depending on you." I pointed between us. "Whatever this is cannot be more important than the dozens of lives we would ruin."

Defeat marred his features. "Aspen, don't just say no. Think about it. Let's—"

"If you respect me, you will let me go and be with someone who can give me all of themselves and not hide me away in some country house," I told him.

Physical pain tore through our bond. He staggered backward, his back hitting the wall as if I'd physically repelled him. "You're right." His voice was monotone. "You deserve better."

It felt like déjà vu. Hadn't I just had a similar conversation with Sterling a few weeks ago? Yet here I was with another man who couldn't commit to me. Even if it wasn't his fault.

There was nothing more to say, so I spun from him, buttoned my shorts, and walked out of the shower soaking wet.

This grief might just be too much for me to bear.

THE NEXT FEW days I sulked around the guest house with Sage, Demi, and Liv. I'd told them what had transpired between Luka and I and they were all heartbroken for my situation, but understood Luka becoming king was the highest priority.

"I had to play the game in order to get Sawyer. The stupid bylaws and rules these old werewolves and vampires put into place are ridiculous," Demi told me, which made me feel a little better. It was a whole new culture and I was just going to have to let his life with Cassara play out. If they had a family together, I wouldn't break that up. I needed to move on. But the shower played out in my mind all day long for days on end.

I pushed it aside, and made sure that when Luka came over for feedings the girls were present and he drank from my wrist. Because of the complicated feelings between us, it didn't feel nearly as good as it normally did.

Today Liv had accompanied him to an event posing as a feeder even though he'd secretly fed from me before. Now I was sitting around with Demi and Sage planning our eventual attack on the breeder encampment, waiting for Liv to come back.

"Where will they go when we free them?" I suddenly asked, wondering where my mother and probably sister would live. They might be able to live in Spokane, but other hunter factions would probably go after them for being part fey if they found out. Were all the hunter factions part fey? They had to be in order to have the strength and speed and other abilities, right? I had more questions than I had answers.

My mind chewed on this while Demi spoke: "They would be welcomed in Wolf City. Many of the supernatural races live there."

Relief washed over me at that. "Thank you."

The door opened and Liv stepped inside.

"How'd it go?" I asked, jumping up from my spot on the carpet.

Liv's eyes were wide. "Luka is a *maniac* fighter. He won."

We all sighed with relief. I guess pent-up rage and a stint in prison had its benefits.

Because two of the vampires had abdicated the throne, the entire timeline had been moved up. Luka's final fight would be in a few days, and then the victor would be announced. "Who is the final fight between? Who is left?" I asked eagerly.

Liv swallowed hard. "Morgana."

I visibly winced, my body flinching. Morgana was a wild card. She was powerful and just psycho enough to do something crazy.

"He'll win," Demi assured us.

Liv chewed her lip nervously as if something else were on her mind.

"What is it?" I asked.

My bestie sighed. "Morgana is already married and has two heirs. By law, Luka can't enter the final fight without a wife, so…"

My eyebrows hit my hairline. "So?"

Liv looked down at her clasped hands, resigned. "He is to marry Cassara tomorrow night in a small ceremony."

I swayed, the shock of her words slashing into me painfully.

"No," I whispered, even though I knew it must happen. But I wasn't expecting it so soon.

Demi and Sage stepped into my side and each slung an arm around my shoulders.

Tears filled Liv's eyes as she spoke again. "And

Luka and Cassara must have an heir within a year or the vampire council will abdicate to Morgana."

I ripped myself away from the comfort of Demi and Sage and burst down the hall to my room, a sob shoved so painfully into my throat that I couldn't breathe.

"Aspen!" Liv called after me.

The moment I got inside, I locked the door and threw myself onto the bed, weeping into my pillow.

This was what I got for falling for a vampire. And I couldn't even leave, I was bound to him for life. The depression of that fully settled into my bones. I couldn't leave, but I couldn't fully be with him. What a horrible juxtaposition.

I lay there a long time just staring at the ceiling and ignoring the soft knocks that came at my door. I was considering going back out to the girls and asking them to watch a movie, when my burner phone rang inside my backpack.

I stilled.

Only one person had this number. Sterling. And he was dead.

With a shaky hand, I unzipped the pack and pulled out the phone, seeing that the number was unlisted.

"Hello." My voice shook as I answered the call.

"Oh good, you're still alive. Lay low, I will be in

touch," a familiar female voice said before the line went dead.

I pulled the phone back and stared at the screen in shock.

Why would Ruby Thorn call me, and how did she get this number?

My mind spun. Did Sterling contact Ruby? Did Vasquez? Was Ruby in with Maz, or was she an outlier like me?

The sun set as my mind tried to work out all of the details and think up what this could possibly mean. I lay there for hours until I finally got up and slipped into sleep shorts and drifted off to sleep.

I AWOKE TO A TAPPING NOISE. It wouldn't stop and it pulled me from a deep sleep. The window. Someone was tapping on the window, I realized. Sitting up, I pried my eyes open and looked at the alarm clock blearily. It was 4 a.m. With a groan, I shuffled over to the window and parted the curtains.

Luka.

He stood in the garden, pleading with his eyes for me to open the window.

I did. But only six inches.

"What's going on?" I asked, the grogginess still fading from my bones.

Luka looked up at me with a pained expression. "Do you want me to marry her? Because say the word and I will leave all of this. We can find another way to save your mom and the breeding farm, and me and my friends can live on the run forever. It doesn't matter."

With that, all the sleep fled from me and I was suddenly alert. "*No*. Then Morgana will become queen and go to war with the werewolves again. You and Walsh, and the rest of Five Crew might get caught one day and thrown back in jail, and we might not have enough forces to save my mom with the werewolves alone."

He looked completely distraught, sagging into himself. "But I don't love her. I don't *want* to marry her."

Hearing him say it simultaneously made me happy and sad at the same time.

I nodded, my throat tightening with emotion. "And yet you must." I barely got the words out before I had to swallow a sob.

He looked off into the moonlit garden as if pondering everything, and I sat on the windowsill, pushing it open all the way as I studied the sharp lines of his face. I was reminded how the water trailed down it as he kissed me in that shower.

He looked up at me then. "I want to have my cake and eat it too." His eyes flared yellow.

"Doesn't everyone want that?" Denial was a nice place to live, but I wanted to stay firmly in reality.

He rushed forward, bracing himself on the ledge as he pulled his body in line with mine and leaned on the windowsill. Our faces were mere inches away from each other and my breath hitched.

"Don't give up on me. I'm going to marry Cassara and become king. But the second your mom is free, the second I pardon my friends, I'm going to have you. *All of you.* I promise." His voice was throaty and it made my stomach do flip flops.

I hated that he was promising me something he couldn't give. I wouldn't fall for another man with empty promises.

"You barely know me, Luka. I'm not worth the trouble."

I looked away from him and stared at the wall, wishing he would just go. I'd already grieved him and now he was giving me hope.

"Hey, look at me." There was hurt in his voice, and when I turned to look at him his eyes were stormy and slitted into a half glare. "I *know* you. Don't ever say that again. I feel you inside of me every single day." He tapped his chest, no doubt referring to the bond.

I swallowed hard, trying not to swoon at the romantic words he was spouting.

"Promise me you won't give up hope. I need something to look forward to if I'm going to marry Cassara." His voice was deep and full of discontent.

I couldn't imagine getting married to someone against my wishes, someone who had been arranged as my life partner since birth. My heart hurt for Luka and his situation, but I also needed to protect myself and my own feelings. "Okay. I won't give up hope," I lied.

Luka and I were doomed from the start. Like a train wreck in slow motion, we were bound to crash eventually.

He pushed off the windowsill and jumped back to the ground. He must have sensed through our bond that I wasn't very serious, because he walked away with his head hung low.

I had never felt more like shit.

I wasn't going to be able to go to sleep after that. Curse this undead man and his wooing ways! *Don't give up hope.* He was asking me to wait for him. What, he was going to marry Cassara, become king, and then divorce her? Then, without heirs, another vampire with children would just take over. Morgana of all people!

Stupid man with his stupid promises.

THE NEXT DAY I spent the entire time bingeing movies with Sage and Demi while Luka married Cassara. I could feel the moment he did it. A deep, soul crushing depression and resignation rushed through our bond and into me. Now it was done and they were spending their honeymoon together, and tomorrow he would fight Morgana to be king.

"Any news on the breeder farm?" I asked Demi, trying to keep my mind occupied.

Demi shook her head. "They are staying put for now, which is good news. My spies say the women seem to be going about their daily routine."

Daily slave routine she meant. That was a comfort, sort of.

I couldn't get the woman's face out of my head, the one who looked like my mother, and the teenager with her.

"I'm going to head to bed," I told the girls, and they all wished me a good night. I just wanted to sleep this funky mood away and prepare for what tomorrow would bring.

I took a long, hot shower before slipping into pj's and then finally shuffled into my room. When I stepped inside, I noticed a note on the bed next to a little box.

Crossing the room, I opened the note and read it.

I GOT this made for you in Werewolf City. That's why I was there with Sawyer the other day. Wait for me. I know you.

-Luka

I RAISED ONE EYEBROW. He got me a gift and gave it to me on *his* wedding night? I wasn't sure what to make of that, or his message to wait for him. I opened the box and looked at what seemed to be a charm bracelet. I pulled it out and inspected it further, unable to help the smile that graced my lips. It had a baby yellow VW Beetle charm hanging from a thick silver chain. I glanced closer at the other charms and full-on laughed. A vampire stake. An Oreo cookie. A tall stiletto boot.

Wait for me. I know you.

He *did* know me, through this bond, through our time together. My heart felt like it was being pinched in a vise with the immeasurable amount of grief I felt at knowing I'd fallen for a man I couldn't have. At least not right now. I decided right then that if God wanted us to be together, he would find a way, and waiting for a little bit wouldn't hurt. Slipping on the charm bracelet, I fell into bed and stared at the ceiling. As my consciousness was drifting into nothingness, I heard his deep voice pierce my awareness.

'I wish it were you,' Luka said as I glided into a deep sleep.

I PUSHED the food around my plate while I ate breakfast with the girls.

*'This might be a stupid question, but is there a church
in Vampire City? I'd like to pray for you before your big
fight.'* I pressed the thought along to Luka through
our bond. I was a nervous wreck thinking about this
final fight with Morgana and all it would mean. We
hadn't spoken about the wedding and I'd rather we
not, but I could use some spiritual uplifting.

*'Not a stupid question, but no church. The undead
tend to avoid those places.'*

I chuckled to myself. I figured as much.

"What if Luka loses? He's fighting Morgana and
she's hardcore," Sage said, breaking my thoughts
away from praying for Luka. She dipped a piece of
bacon into her syrup and popped it into her mouth.

Gunner had slipped in early and worked hard to cook a five-course breakfast for us all. The dude had grown on me. He reminded me so much of my beloved Kenz.

"*Luka* is hardcore, he goes all psycho like an ex-con with daddy issues," Liv told the table, which caused Demi to burst into laughter.

"I mean, that's not far off." The alpha took a bite of her eggs.

I remembered, seeing how he'd snapped on Nico and said it was for his sister.

"I think they did something to his family. He has a reason to be angry." I wanted to defend him.

Demi nodded, face suddenly serious. "Sawyer told me it's bad … whatever it is, whatever they did … it almost broke him."

My heart squeezed. I wanted to know more but also didn't want to pry.

"They're all sick if you ask me. The entire Drake line. Other than Luka of course," Sage said, drinking some orange juice.

Demi nodded in agreement. "They have a freaky breeding farm similar to the one we're going to raid in a few days."

Was Luka born out of love, or just to produce a certain set of genes? He'd indicated he'd been changed into a vampire against his will. I wondered who changed him and what did that do to a person? To be turned into a creature that feeds off of blood for the rest of their life without consent? It would make me dark too—I'd want revenge, which is what I was sure this was. Nico was revenge for something done to his sister, and hopefully Luka would trust me enough one day to tell me.

"If the fight looks like it's going south, do we have a plan?" I raised one eyebrow. Luka was an amazing fighter, but if it looked like Morgana was winning, I wanted some assurance that Luka wouldn't be killed.

Demi nodded. "Sawyer and I have agreed that if it looked like Luka is losing … I'll step in and we all go on the run."

Holy wow.

I hadn't really seen Demi in action, but I'd heard stories, and if she was going to get involved it would be a bloodbath.

"There are hundreds of vampires in that room. We'd never make it out alive," I told her honestly.

Demi clenched her jaw and nodded. "Then let's hope he wins."

Maybe with the four of us fighting we could escape. He'd have to live on the run, and my mom wouldn't be freed as easily, but he'd be alive. I could live with that, especially now that I was sure that I'd stupidly fallen in love with him.

"Shall we?" Demi stood and wiped her mouth.

I'd barely eaten, I was too nervous for him. I simply nodded and stood as well. Demi adjusted her wrist cuffs, making sure they were firmly secured. Then we put away our plates and stepped outside to join the throngs of people. Hundreds of vampires walked in long, single-file lines to gain entry into the building where the final fight was being held. They were a people without a leader and this would set them on a path that they would follow for as long as that leader lived. Which could be forever. Or in Luka's case, however long I would live.

I'd never been surrounded by so many bloodsuckers in my entire life. My body tensed with each one that passed by, and I noticed the same reaction in my female companions. Demi, Liv, and Sage were all clearly feeling the same sort of unease as I was.

After checking in with the guard at the front, we were asked to sit in the feeder corner with the others. Huddling our chairs together, I bopped my foot nervously as more and more vampires flooded the space and filled the bleachers. The floor around the mat was bursting with vampires standing and craning their necks to get an eyeful of Luka and Morgana. The two royal members sat on a specially erected stage, just next to the elder vamps, who looked a hundred years old but were probably ten times that.

Luka looked calm and slightly annoyed as Cassara hung on his arm, stroking his bicep, her giant diamond ring glistening in the overhead lighting.

Kill me now.

Did they sleep together last night? Their wedding night. Of course they did. Pain pressed in on me as I thought of him having sex with her—doing to her what he did to me in the shower the other day. Being so intimate with someone who he supposedly didn't even like … it sickened me a bit but I swallowed that feeling down.

"Miss Rose?" Gunner's voice snapped me from my thoughts as both Liv and I turned to him. "Luka has requested you meet him in the feeding room."

I swallowed hard, looking back at the space Luka had been sitting to find it empty. Instead I was met with another set of eyes. Cassara glared at me across the arena and I gulped, standing.

Walking through the large ballroom, I let myself out into the hallway and then over to the doors where the feeding rooms were. Once I was standing in front of the door that bore Luka's name, I took in a deep breath to steady my nerves.

He married her … after what we did in the shower he married her. I'd told him to … but still … I hadn't thought it would hurt this badly.

You idiot! This guy will destroy you! my heart was screaming at me. But I couldn't help but turn the knob and step inside. The moment I closed the door behind me, my eyes adjusted to the light and then Luka was before me. He reached up with his hands and cupped my face, bringing my lips close to his.

"You're all I've thought about day and night," he murmured, his breath washing over my face and causing my body to melt into his. I reached up and threaded my fingers over his, stopping when I felt the cold chill of metal. Pulling back, I looked down at the wedding band on his ring finger and a whimper died in my throat.

"I can't, Luka. Not while you're married. It goes against my morals." I dropped his hand and stepped away from him.

He nodded once, his face devoid of emotion. "I respect that. Can I assume that since you're wearing the bracelet I gave you, it means you'll wait a little while? That you trust me to figure this out?"

I looked down at the yellow VW Beetle charm and nodded. "A little while."

I owed him that. I owed *us* that.

A full-fledged grin graced his face, and holy hell it made him so much more beautiful. Luka Drake was off-the-charts sexy.

I gave him my wrist, the one that held the charm bracelet, and pressed it to his mouth. There was a pinch of pain before the pleasure ebbed into me mixed with a tumult of confusion. I didn't know where we stood and that made the feedings all the more awkward. He pulled away after a moment and licked my wrist, sending a sensual tingle down my spine. Leaning forward, he brushed his cheek against mine and whispered into my ear. "I haven't touched Cassara. I told her I was too stressed with the fight and she slept in her own room."

Surprise rushed through me, then he pulled away, planting a light kiss on my nose, and left.

He hadn't touched her … but how long would she be okay with that type of arrangement? Not to mention I doubted the marriage was legal if it wasn't consummated quickly.

Still … his bold act told me something.

Luka Drake cared for me far more than I expected. It meant the world to me when people I could trust with my heart were in short supply.

. . .

AFTER QUICKLY RETURNING to my seat, I made it just in time to hear the announcer invite Luka and Morgana to the ring. The space was about four times that of a wrestling ring you would see on TV, but it had the same mats and expandable strings around the edge. This was a different setup than the one with Nico and the others. I wondered if Luka was going to go for no weapons again this time, but instead he wisely grabbed two. A silver stake and a long sword, fit for a king. The handle glinted off the light, revealing gold, silver and a few precious gems.

Once the two had stepped into the ring, the announcer bellowed. "Place all final bets!"

I glanced out at the crowd as people rushed to a makeshift betting booth that had been set up.

"This is sickening," Sage growled from her place beside Liv and I.

"Now remember what makes this fight so unique," the announcer continued, "is that Morgana sired Luka and so he *cannot* kill her. Whether she wins or loses, she will be walking away with her life today. I can't say the same for Luka."

The crowd roared, but Sage, Demi, Liv and I all physically stiffened. Morgana could walk away from this even if she lost the fight? She was the one who changed Luka against his will?

My gaze flicked to Luka to find him shooting eye daggers at Morgana. She forcibly changed him and then tried to kill him at Bang? What a psycho.

'Kick her royal ass,' I seethed through our bond.

He glanced at me, throwing me a halfcocked grin. *'Gladly, my love.'*

My love. Those words slipped off his tongue so easily and yet they had so much impact. My entire body felt like it had suddenly become so light that I might just fly up to the ceiling.

My love. It wasn't "I love you," but it was close.

Whatever fun, carefree, and sexy thing Luka and I had going, it had grown much deeper, more permanent. Neither of us would come out of this unscathed at this point, and I was okay with that. Such was the gamble with any relationship.

But this one felt like the stakes were just a bit higher.

"I made you and I can end you. Don't forget that," Morgana suddenly bellowed across the mat, and the crowd went crazy.

"You're lucky I can't kill you," Luka spat back.

"Well, well, the trash talking has begun. Let's get this started, shall we?" the announcer asked the crowd. They stomped their feet and shouted until their voices were hoarse.

One of the elder vampires stood and a meek looking vampire scurried over to him with a microphone. A hush fell over the crowd.

The elder male was wearing a long, red, crushed velvet cloak and looked familiar, but I couldn't place him. He wasn't a Drake, but he was important.

"Drucilla Drake was a steadfast and fearsome leader, and she will be missed, but she led us into a war that will take some time to recover from."

Oh, that was kind of a burn. Demi looked at me as if to confirm I had heard that and interpreted it the same, and I gave her a curt nod.

"It will be nice to have a fresh sense of leadership!" His voice was smooth, direct, and to the point. He was totally on Luka's side.

I grinned as the assembled crowd clapped. Sage reached out and grasped Demi's hand; Liv grabbed mine and we all held our breaths.

"Winner takes the crown," the elder vampire bellowed. "Now fight!"

The final word had barely left his lips when Luka was a blur on the mat. He tore across the space, weapons raised. Morgana planted her feet, squatting into a defensive position. She hissed, white knuckling the axe and sword in her iron grip. Right before Luka reached her, Morgana made an X with her weapons and Luka crashed into her, sending her flying backward. She crashed into the mats and I noticed a thin bead of blood dotted her arm, but nothing more. Quickly, she popped right back up. They traded blow for blow, weapons clacking with such force I feared they would snap in half.

It felt like I didn't breathe for a full two minutes, I just froze and watched the impressive display of power before me. Every time Luka would throw a blow, Morgana would block it with a weapon and counterattack. I was pretty sure I was breaking Liv's hand with how hard I was holding it. I was just starting to wonder if either would actually win this, when Luka came down hard on Morgana's axe handle and severed the metal head clean off. It fell to the floor with a clunk and the crowd went wild. Using that distraction, Luka smashed his forehead into Morgana's nose. The crack of bone shattering rang throughout the space and the assembled crowd amplified their screams of maniacal joy.

My gaze flicked to the bleachers, where Cassara bopped in her chair with excitement, and I wondered how much of it was for Luka's success, or her chance to become queen.

In a blur of movement, Morgana used the close proximity to take the shorn-off wooden axe handle and slam it right into Luka's ribcage. A yelp ripped from my throat, terror rushing through me as Luka nearly flew backward and out of harm's way. The wooden handle protruded from his side, and anxiety firmly clutched me in its grips. Sage reached out to Liv and clutched her hand so that we were all forming some kind of anxiety prayer ring for Luka as we watched the fight unfold.

Luka grasped the handle of the wooden stick, yanking it out cleanly as Morgana chose that moment to advance again.

My gaze flicked to the side to see Demi drop Sage's hand and place her fingers on the edge of her cuffs, ready to flip them off and intervene. Those cuffs kept her powers at bay, but also kept the vampires from smelling whatever she was.

A split shifter, Sage had called her? I didn't know the details, but I knew if she pulled those cuffs off, we would have a big problem. Every vampire in the room would smell her fancy blood and it would be hell to get out of here after that. The guards at the door made sure we had no weapons, so fighting our way out was the last resort.

"Give him a chance," I told her and she froze, looking sideways at me. "Trust me."

She didn't feel the absolute power and rage coming off of Luka like I did. He had Morgana right where he wanted her. I sensed not even an ounce of fear or resignation.

Our gazes went back to the mat as we watched Luka stand tall in proud defiance. He let Morgana come to him, unmoving, unflinching as she let out a battle roar, raising her sword.

What was he doing!? He wasn't even raising his weapons. Had he lost his mind? I wanted to say something mentally, but I didn't want to distract him, so I just gripped Liv's and Sage's hands until I was sure I might be breaking them. A millisecond before Morgana reached him, Luka crouched and then leaped into the air like a freaking ninja. Morgana passed through empty space as he sailed over her head, spinning in midair. With her back to him, Luka reached out and drove the stake right into the side of *her* ribcage. Matching his wound. It wasn't enough to kill her, which was apparently against the rules, but he'd made his point. He could have had he wanted to.

The crowd went insane. It was both a good hit and also a show of defiance that he'd marked her equally to him. I burst to my feet screaming and clapping as a demonic look of fury washed over Morgana's face.

She ignored the stake lodged in her side and swung blindly, clipping Luka's forearm, causing him to drop his sword. Fresh crimson spattered the mat and he winced, retreating backward.

"I taught you everything you know!" she roared as she stalked after him. "Don't think I don't know all your tricks."

Luka sneered at her, pulling his lips back to display his canines. "The only thing you taught me is what it's like to be raised by a coldhearted *bitch*."

A hushed silence fell over the crowd as we witnessed this personal moment. Morgana raised him?

Holy crap.

Her head reeled back as if she'd been slapped. "Your mother was too soft on you. You'd be a weak teddy bear if you'd have been left with her."

"If you let her live, you mean?" Luka's voice was absolutely venomous.

The crowd gasped at his declaration and Morgana stilled. "I would never. My own sister." But her voice shook a little when she said it.

"But you convinced my father, didn't you?" His voice could cut glass, and as I sifted through his emotions, I felt that he'd wanted to ask her this for so long. Wanting to know. I wanted to know what

Morgana convinced his father of, that much was certain.

Did this woman kill his mom and force change him to make him into some strong vampire?

"Cut her heart out!" I screamed at the top of my lungs, and the crowd roared their approval.

Luka smirked, and then all hell broke loose.

The two vampires ran at each other with so much force and speed that the mats slipped and shook like an earthquake were erupting under their feet.

He had no weapon, and yet I felt through the bond that he had enough to kill her with his anger alone. He wore that fury both like weapon and shield, and I'd never felt prouder. Years had led up to and culminated to this point, and he was finally going to get peace over it. I felt everything he felt, like he was purposefully opening up and sharing it with me.

When they crashed into each other, there was a tumble too fast for my eyes to track, and then Morgana's sword fell away from her, clattering outside the ring.

When they stopped moving, Morgana was on her knees, face red, Luka stood behind her with her neck clasped in his hands. He was going to rip her head off. The realization hit me and I flinched, preparing for it. Just as his biceps flexed to yank her head right off, she opened her mouth.

"I submit!" she wheezed.

Pure unbridled rage flooded Luka's face and his grip tightened as he twisted her head slightly, adjusting his grip. Holy crap … I thought he wasn't allowed to.

"Luka Drake!" one of the elders suddenly stood and screamed. "You will honor the Sire-Fledgling pact or you will have no place as king!"

Luka took three deep breaths, which was saying a lot since vampires didn't need to breathe, and then he released her head.

The crowd went absolutely crazy, clapping, cheering, throwing people and objects into the air.

The announcer pulled the microphone to her lips and grinned. "May I introduce your new king, Luka Drake. Long may he reign."

"Long may he reign!" the crowd shouted, and then broke into chants.

Morgana stood, a smug smile at her lips, and limped over to where her husband was seated.

Luka was still, his side wound and arm still weeping, slowed by the silver that was imbedded into the weapons. He wore an unreadable expression, and I wasn't sure if he was proud of his accomplishment or saddened by it.

Shaking himself from his stoic appearance, he plastered on a smile and raised his hand into the air, which set the crowd off into another fit of cheers and throwing people and things. They were frantic, maniacal.

'Bring Liv so it's not suspicious and meet me in the feeder room,' he told me, and stepped offstage to be kissed and cooed over by Cassara.

I grasped Liv's hand and motioned to the exit. "Feeder room," I told her.

She nodded, totally getting my meaning.

Demi was wearing a grin. "I'm going to spread the good news to Sawyer. I'll meet you back at the guest house." Clearly she was overjoyed by the win, as I should be, but I couldn't get over the sadness I felt that Luka was unable to take Morgana down and avenge his mother or whatever had happened to her.

Liv and I made quick work crossing the hallway and stepping into the feeding room. I slipped into Luka's little closet while Liv waited outside. He opened the door on the adjoining wall, which I now saw was linked to the locker rooms we'd been in the other day. Seeing a glimpse of the showers made me blush.

The second he closed the door, I shoved my wrist in his face. "Drink. You're hurt."

He shook his head. "I drank from you right before. I'll be fine."

I frowned. "No, *I'll* be fine. Drink."

He shook his head. "I just wanted to see you." He reached out and trailed his finger down my cheek and into the curve of my neck, causing goosebumps to race down my spine.

I stepped forward seductively, knowing that in order to get him to drink, I'd have to force his hand. I pulled my long red hair over one shoulder and exposed my neck, stepping onto my tippy toes and shoving it in his face.

"Aspen," he growled.

"I want it," I begged, and it wasn't a lie.

With a snarl, his face shot forward and there was a pinch at my neck as his teeth slid into my vein. Raw pleasure burst to life throughout my body and I clung to him, moaning as he drank from me.

'You taste like heaven,' he murmured. *'Like honey, white chocolate, and sunshine.'*

I grinned, chuckling at that description just as he pulled away and licked my neck. The pad of his tongue stroked my skin and I moaned again. A flicker of sadness crossed his face and I frowned.

"What?" I asked.

He shook his head. "Morgana. I was hoping I

could kill her today and the elders would overlook the Sire-Fledgling Pact."

I grimaced. "So you can't ever kill her. *Ever*?"

"Vampire law will forbid me from it."

"How will they know?"

"Witches. They can see everything you do, play back your memories like they were a movie."

Holy crap.

"Did she kill your mother?" I asked boldly. "You want to avenge her?"

He stilled. "It's a long story, but she had a hand in it. Among other unspeakable things."

"Then I'll do it," I declared and he went stock still. "Asp—"

"One day, when circumstances allow, *I* will avenge your mother. I swear it on God's holy name," I professed, and his eyes glistened with unshed tears.

"I couldn't ask you to—"

"She's evil. I'm a hunter. Let me right the wrongs of all the innocents I've probably killed by actually taking out a bad one."

He reached up and cupped my face, leaning his forehead on mine. "I wished it were you. All last night when I was standing there taking my vows to Cassara, I just kept picturing *you*."

My heart skipped a beat. I wanted to cry at such a

declaration and the cruel fate we'd been given, but I forced myself to focus on the good.

"You're king now. Let's not make it all be for nothing."

His eyes blazed yellow. "Oh, it will be for everything. I'll pardon the boys and have your mother back by the end of the week. I *promise*." He kissed my nose again, tenderly, and my heart ached to be with him. It was torture seeing him married to Cassara. Pulling back, he looked me in the eyes and what felt like right down into the depths of my soul.

"Aspen Rose…" He paused. "I—"

There was a hard triple knock on the door, my code with Liv, and I jerked away from Luka just as the door wrenched open.

"Are you done?" Cassara's voice held a subtle threat. Luka wiped his mouth and gave her a glare that would stop me in my tracks.

"Yes, *darling*," he all but growled.

"Oh good. I'm ready to consummate this marriage," she purred over my shoulder, and my whole body tensed. I didn't dare turn around, I didn't want her to see the tears rolling down my cheeks.

Luka took one look at me and a gutted expression graced his face before it was gone under a mask of calm.

Without another word, he stepped out of the feeding booth and walked away with her. The moment I heard the door close behind them, I slid against the wall and to the ground of the feeding room, bursting into sobs.

Liv stepped inside, closed the door, and sat next to me, wrapping her arms around me as I cried. I cried for Sterling, I cried for Luka, I cried for my horrible choices in men and that I always fell for the wrong guy. I cried so hard my voice was hoarse by the end of it.

"You fell in love with him, didn't you?" Liv asked softly.

I hadn't admitted this fully to myself until now. All I could do was nod my head.

She sighed, wrapping me tighter in her arms. "You just had to go and fall in love with a betrothed vampire king, didn't you?"

My sobs turned into laughter, which she matched, before mine turned back into pathetic sobs.

"I'm telling you, we need normal guys. Like—"

"Accountants and engineers?"

She nodded. "Accountants and engineers don't go becoming vampire kings."

It was true. I had a broken guy finder. Mine went

to the hottest, most emotionally unavailable man in the vicinity and latched on for dear life.

"He's king. You've done your part. Now we save the breeder slaves and then go back to Spokane and find *normal* guys. Then we can try to take down Maz and get revenge for everything she did to us," Liv said.

I nodded, but knew in my heart it wouldn't be that easy.

Wait for me, his letter had said, and I was going to do just that … wait as long as my heart could bear.

DEMI PULLED me in for a hug. "Aww, I don't want to say goodbye, this has been so fun!"

I peered past her at her husband. The werewolf alpha was wearing his adorable baby boy in a carrier on his chest as he stood waiting for his wife in front of her white Range Rover. Walsh stood proudly beside him, in full view of everyone and no longer in hiding. Luka was crowned king three days ago and he'd exonerated his friends immediately. Now he was calling for an army of volunteers to free the breeder slaves from the clutches of the fey.

The Elder Council approved his request to lead a contingent up into fey territory, without warning them, on the stipulation that any and all warriors were volunteers for the cause. And that any blowback, like war declared on the vampires, would be shared between the werewolves. It meant that if anyone attacked the vamps, Sawyer and Demi would come out in droves to protect them. It was the first real peace accord between the two races in hundreds of years and everyone seemed pretty excited about it.

There were scowls here and there when Demi walked past, or when the vamps saw Sawyer drive in like he owned the place and hug Luka like they were brothers, but for the most part the vampires here seemed to crave change. Morgana had fled back to Spokane and I would keep my promise to wipe her from the face of the Earth the moment I got my new hunter guild up and running. She would be my first kill, a truly evil woman I had witnessed with my own two eyes.

Demi pulled away after a while and then I hugged Sage tightly.

"You better be at my wedding!" she declared.

I laughed. "I'm so there."

"Me too!" Liv tackle-hugged us, squishing me between them both.

Someone crashed into my back and squeezed, and I laughed when I looked back and saw Demi getting in on our little hug sandwich.

Demi's son let loose with a wail then and Sawyer cleared his throat. "Creek wants his mama."

Demi pulled away from us and approached her

son, cooing as she plucked him out of the carrier, smothering his face with kisses.

Sage winked at me. "We will meet at the rendezvous tomorrow night."

Yes. In twenty-four hours we would team up with the wolves and free all those women. Demi's spies, AKA Bennet and Talon, had followed them to their new location at the edge of the Dark Woods, deep in Dark Fey Territory. They had moved, just as we had thought, but we'd followed them the entire way.

Excitement and apprehension thrummed through me at the thought of meeting my mom.

"See you tomorrow," I told them.

Tomorrow night, I took a little something back from Maz for everything she'd taken from me.

I'D NEVER BEEN to war. I'd killed nearly a hundred vampires but it wasn't *war*. Now as I sat inside of a legit war bus that was ferrying us through enemy lands, I wasn't sure I was ready. How in God's name did my life get to this point? One day I'm praying to expunge every evil vampire from Earth and the next I'm in love with one and following his people into a battle to save my mother…

My mother who is a slave at a fey breeding farm.

I mean, at what point did I just break down and see a therapist? This couldn't be healthy to go through so much change all at once, so fast.

I reached out and tapped my back pocket, feeling some relief at the burner phone there. I'd been waiting for Ruby to call me back. Something told me when she did, it was going to change everything and I'd get some of the answers I was seeking.

Liv got up from our shared bus seat, pulling me from my thoughts, and Luka slipped into the open seat beside me. My whole body reacted to being in this close of a proximity to him, heating up and leaning toward him in the hopes that our arms would brush each other or something silly like that.

He turned and looked down at me, eyes scanning over my weapons cache. It felt weird not to have any stakes, but such a thing was not needed with fey. I had two katanas crossed in an X at my back, one Glock in a thigh holster on my right leg, and over half a dozen throwing stars in my waist belt. To top it all off, I was wearing a thin chainmail long-sleeve top Luka had sent for me. These witches were going to drown in their own evil black blood.

'Please be safe. Stay behind the front lines of my men,' Luka's voice whispered in my head.

We couldn't speak freely here with so many in earshot. Supernatural earshot no less.

I gave him a cocky grin. *'I'm a supernatural hunter, Luka. I'll be fine.'*

He rubbed his face, looking stressed. We hadn't spoken about things since Cassara had so aptly declared she wanted to consummate their marriage. I knew he was playing the role he needed to in order to be the king we all needed him to be. I just tried not to think about the details.

He looked so damn sexy in his all-black battle gear. I just wanted to be with him, freely, no secret kisses in the feeder closet, which I'd stopped doing now that he was married. Fake marriage or not, it felt wrong.

I stared at the gold wedding band on his left hand and guilt gnawed at my gut. What if she loved him? Truly loved him, and wasn't just trying to be queen and gain power?

I'm the other woman. That was so wrong and against every moral pillar I'd built my life on.

His hand snaked out and slid over my thigh, but I pulled away from him.

'Did you figure out the stuff with Cassara?' I asked boldly. *'What you're going to do?'*

His hurt at my rejection filtered through our bond, but he pulled his hand back and set it on his lap.

'I'm working on multiple strategies.'

What did that mean? Either he was going to divorce her after we raided this fey slave camp or I was out. I'd still feed him to keep him alive, but nothing more.

I leaned my head against the windowpane, watching the trees and straw huts go past. We were on some old dirt road, and with each bounce my head knocked against the window.

Luka leaned in, pressing his body against the side of mine and whispered into my ear. "I need you to trust me." His breath feathered over me, before he stood and walked back to the front.

Trust. Something that was in short supply after being lied to my entire life and basically joining a cult.

Liv slipped back into her seat at my side and gave me a sympathetic look. She'd had to deal with all my tears over this man and all I could do was pray it ended in a happy story. Otherwise it was just too depressing.

Luka stood at the front and cleared his throat. "I will not ask you to mindlessly fight in my name without knowing what you are fighting for. Drucilla was a fearsome leader but she fought wars for her own gain. I will not do that." The vampires slapped their hands on their seat tops to make a noise of agreement.

"The women and children we are about to free are innocents," he growled. "My informant tells me they are shackled, some of them pregnant, and have been forced against their will to sell their babies for a profit they clearly do not see." The bus exploded in an uproar of angry snarls, and I saw the wisdom in asking only people who had volunteered on this journey. They were doing it for the right reasons.

"We will rip apart the fey who imprison these women!" Luka yelled, and the vampires pounded on the seats, showing their agreement as tears pricked the edges of my eyes. Liv reached out and grasped my hand and I knew she was feeling the same pride for Luka as I was.

Whatever became of he and I, him becoming king was the most important thing I ever could have helped with.

Luka stepped forward, clearly not done. "These women will be given back their lives, in a joint venture with the werewolves, because the new Vampire City that I intend to create as king is one that will be built on a strong moral foundation."

His eyes met mine then and I smiled, my heart absolutely beaming with respect and pride. The bus erupted into screams of agreement, Liv and mine included, as we drove deeper into the Dark Fey Territory. The werewolves were right behind us.

This was a joint venture, the dawn of a new age here in Magic City, where the peace between the werewolves and vampires would hold.

We spent the next hour driving. We passed villages full of fey that came out to stare at us. They looked like simple people carrying baskets of food and doing housework. But as I peered closer, I noticed one woman doing tarot card readings, and at one point I peered into a tent and noticed some crystal shards and the dead claw foot of a chicken. They reminded me of witches. I shivered, saying a quick prayer of protection. Luka didn't seem worried about letting the fey know we were in their territory. I guessed it was because they were so behind the times. Not a cell phone or car in sight. By the time one of them rode a horse to the main city, we would be done. The bus stopped just at the base of a hill and Luka stood, addressing everyone.

"We go the rest of the way on foot. It's right over the hill." Luka indicated to the large grassy mound in the distance.

Liv and I stood, waiting for everyone to exit before we disembarked, filtering out into the wild woodlands as the werewolves did the same. There was a third bus, completely empty, that we hoped would carry the women and children we were about to save. I did a quick headcount, grinning when I tallied over a hundred men and women in all. Our army was equally split between wolves and vampires. Demi and Sage looked badass and battle ready. Sage was in her wolf form, and Demi was already barking orders at her Paladin warriors. She had streaks of blue paint on her face, and had a dagger in a thigh holster on her leg.

Sawyer commanded his city wolves, who started to strip down naked and shift into their animal form. My eyebrows raised in surprise at their lack of regard for their nakedness.

"Werewolves are hot," Liv murmured.

I elbowed her lightly, grinning.

"What?" she said. "If we are okay with dating supernaturals now, I want one of those." She eyed a tall Paladin male with caramel skin and no shirt. His washboard abs were streaked with blue paint; he clutched a spear in his tight grip.

"The Paladins are kind of yummy," I agreed, and Liv smiled.

Luka stepped over to Demi and Sawyer and motioned them to walk over to the spot Liv and I waited, just at the front of the bus.

Luka held a satellite phone in his hand. It was giant and looked like it was from the '80s, but I was guessing cell towers were in short supply in these lands. From what I'd heard, technology was favored by the light fey, not the dark. They despised technology, as did the troll folk.

"When we get over this ridge, I'm going to call the fey leader and give him one chance to give up the breeders without a fight. Otherwise, we go in guns blazing and all but declare war on the fey."

Sawyer and Demi nodded.

"Good plan. Very diplomatic," Demi stated.

Luka gave her a look. "Someone has to be."

She reached out and swatted his head but he grinned. Some might see it as flirting, but I enjoyed their banter. It seemed to be more brotherly to me.

"Stop flirting with my wife," Sawyer growled, causing Luka and Demi to smile.

Called it.

"You do the possessive alpha thing well, my friend," Luka razzed his best friend. "And have no fear. My heart is taken." Luka looked right at me then, and I froze.

Sawyer cracked a smile. "Alright, let's do this."

They started to walk, but I was rooted to the spot. Did Luka just admit in front of his friends that his heart was taken … by me? Surely he was talking about Cassara and only *looked* at me coincidently.

"He totally meant you," Liv said, obviously picking up on my thoughts.

A smile graced my lips and I had to run to keep up with them.

Oh man, I had it bad. So bad.

As we hiked over the hill, wolf and vampire alike, we were one unified army. I could sense the pride in the leaders, at what they had accomplished. Getting the two races together like this, after just being at war, was no small feat. When we reached the peak of the hill, I cast my gaze downward and a stone sank in my gut.

It was … a fortress. Like the ones you saw in old-time movies. High walls with men patrolling the top, and just one double gate, which was sealed shut. Large columns rose up every twenty feet around the wall, and at the top looked to be a bowmen.

"Holy crap, we're dead," I breathed.

Luka frowned. "Looks like they are ready for us. Someone tipped them off."

Demi nodded, rolling out her neck. "Still want to make that call?"

Luka picked up the phone. "I'm guessing it's going to be quick." He dialed a number that was on a piece of paper while the wolves and vampires fanned out on the hillside.

"Yes, hello, Prime Minister, this is Luka Drake, King of the Vampires. I'm here in your territory at the illegal breeder farm—"

He pulled the phone away from his ear then and hung it up, grinning. "He hung up. Let's attack. We have due cause."

"Ready wolves!" Sawyer screamed and his voice was barely human, which caused the hair on my arms to stand up. The wolves howled in response and my stomach flipped over with nerves.

"Vampires at the ready!" Luka shouted, and the bloodsuckers responded with battle cries that would impress even the most seasoned warrior.

"How will we get inside?" I tightened the grip on my knife and eyed the door, the wall, the insane security forces.

Demi grinned as a shadow passed over us, blotting out the sun.

Pearl.

The dragon landed right in front of the entire army. Gasps of awe ripped through the crowd. "We drop down right in the center of the fort and open the gates from the inside," Demi called out. "The army will be ready to charge in and get our back."

'Please stay here behind the front lines,' Luka begged.

"I'm going," I told everyone, and stepped forward to get onto Pearl's back. Luka let loose with a curse word.

"She's a badass. She'll be fine. I'm coming too, by

the way," Liv told Luka, and we mounted Pearl, sitting right behind Marmal.

Demi and Sawyer shared a look with Luka, and Demi nodded. "It's their mothers in there," Demi finally said.

"Fine," Luka grumbled. "But *be safe*," he said to me.

Blah blah was all I heard. I was ready to take some fey heads.

Luka, Demi, Sawyer, and Sage crawled onto Pearl just behind Liv and I. Luka tucked himself directly behind me, straddling my butt as his thighs spread wide and I sank into him.

I had to take in a deep breath to steady my heartbeat and clear my head.

Reaching out, Luka stroked Pearl's scales. "Hello, beautiful. I missed you."

Marmal grinned. "She says hello."

I frowned, curious about when he'd met Pearl before.

"She's how we busted them out of prison," Sage told me, and I nodded in realization.

I could imagine the faces of the jail's guards when a giant dragon flew up to take away a handful of their prisoners.

"Good girl." I patted her gently.

Her wings snapped out then and Demi looked at her second-in-command, the dude she'd called Rab.

"The second those doors open, you be ready!" she screamed.

"Yes, Alpha!" he called back, and pulled a shield from behind his back.

Pearl's wings flapped, and we were airborne.

"They'll have a fey shield up!" Marmal screamed against the wind.

Demi nodded and looked out into the thick forest, scanning for something. A small group of three women stepped out, holding hands.

"Right on time." Demi grinned.

Witches.

I swallowed hard, watching as they chanted under their breath, hands clasped together as they stared up at the top of the fort. They must have a bubble of protection over it, something I certainly couldn't see from here.

My throat tightened with emotion as I realized what great detail had gone into this rescue and what favors they must have had to call in.

"Thank you all! I'll never forget this!" My voice cracked.

Everyone nodded, and Luka reached forward and squeezed my thigh. This time I didn't pull away.

Pearl flew higher into the sky and Luka's voice

came through our bond. *'Please don't get hurt. I would die if anything happened to you.'*

I chuckled, looking back at him. *'Literally.'*

He rolled his eyes. *'That's not what I meant.'*

Reaching out, I laced my fingers through his, leaning into his body. *'I know. I will be safe. I promise.'*

He squeezed my hand, and then I pulled away and reached up, grabbing the end of my swords, loosing them from their sheaths.

A pearlescent dome of protection suddenly appeared before us. Pearl hovered above it. I peered down to see the bowmen looking up at us, ready for the assault. Their gaze shifted and then they glanced down at the field, which was now filling with our combined force. They didn't know which to shoot.

"Did anyone bring a bow?" Sage asked just as one of the fey loosed an arrow.

"I got it." Demi raised her hand and flicked it at the arrow, causing it to change direction.

Holy crap, this woman had all kinds of powers that were not normal for a wolf.

Just then, the witches in the woods screamed a collective cry and the dome shattered, dissolving before us.

"Now!" Marmal shouted and then we dropped. I was airborne for a few inches until Luka grasped my hips with one hand and slammed me back onto

Pearl's back. I grasped one of her horns to steady myself. I muttered a quick thanks and then looked down at the chaos before me. Women and children were running everywhere as Munai and fey soldiers flooded the courtyard.

Pearl slammed her talons onto the earth, landing us right into the middle of the fort, and I wasted no time.

"Happy hunting!" I cried to our group, launching off of the dragon at the first male fey warrior I could see. My sword cut through his neck like butter before my feet even slammed to the ground.

I rushed forward, taking the next fey head on. He wasn't a Munai, no black eyes or weird demon look, but he was still powerful. I had to pivot to the side as his sword came down on mine. The clang of metal rang throughout the courtyard as I pushed him backward toward the gate. With a grunt, I caught him off guard and my blade sank into his stomach, right where the liver was. He dropped to his knees, sputtering, and I pulled my blade free.

"Aspen, open the gate. We will hold them off!" Sawyer cried out, and I turned to see an onslaught of warriors had just crashed into our group, who were now in a little fighting circle surrounded by Munai and fey warriors.

While my crew kept them distracted, I charged

for the gate, which had a giant steel bar latching it closed. Three male fey were standing in front of it, facing me with swords drawn. Three against one.

Awesome.

If I didn't get this door open, my friends and I would no doubt be slaughtered. We needed backup. Now.

Beast mode activated.

I thought of Maz, and of my mom being trapped here, and of puppies left by the side of the road, and every evil thing I could think of, building up the rage inside of me. Then I charged with a battle cry. The two fey on the end each got a throwing star to the neck while I collided with the one in the middle. Our swords clashed as I reached into my thigh holster and pulled out my Glock. Two squeezes later, he was dead on the ground. The two fey I'd thrown stars at were rising now, no longer stunned by my distraction, but I put them down easily. Bullets to the brain. Fey were so much easier to kill than vampires.

"Aspen, look out!" Liv called behind me and I spun just in time for a Munai to skid to a halt before me, the tip of my gun pressed to her chest, indenting the skin there.

"Bye," I whispered, and pulled the trigger.

She dropped to the ground like a sack of bricks

and I turned my attention back toward the door. Holstering my Glock, I spun and grasped the cold steel. I could hear the vampires and wolves outside howling and smashing against the door. I needed to open it, STAT. I didn't dare look behind me to see what kind of battle Luka and the others were fighting. I focused on the task at hand.

With a grunt, I heaved the large piece of metal out of the two brackets holding it and it slid out of its position, falling to the ground. Now that the door was no longer latched, the force of our men on the other side pushing it knocked me backward. I fell into someone's grasp; fingers went around my throat and I was dragged backward away from the advancing horde by my neck. Looking up, I saw the Munai that I'd shot moments ago, a healing red sore on her chest.

Oh crap.

Clearly they had magic I knew nothing about. Kicking off the ground, I flipped backward with all my force, knocking the demon back, and pulled out of her grasp, gasping for air. Pain burned in my throat where she's tried to choke me.

Luka zoomed into view then, pounced on the Munai's chest, and pulled her head off like it was a plastic toy. "Go release the prisoners!" he yelled to me. "Liv. Basement trapdoor!"

I knew he was just trying to get me out of the worst of the fighting, but I didn't waste time chatting. I looked up and around the space, taking in all of the doorways that might lead to a basement.

Holy hell.

It was a full-on war.

Sage and Sawyer were ripping people to shreds in their wolf form, while Demi was knocking fey back with some powerful force field stuff. The wolves and vampires tore into the fey, but they just kept coming.

I spotted a door at the far wall that led to some kind of underground basement or root cellar and saw Liv already running for it.

Bingo.

Bursting from where I stood, I booked it in and out of the crowd, meeting Liv at the padlocked door. A dead Munai was crumpled in front of it, her head a few feet from her body.

"You have to behead them like vamps or shoot them in the brain. They are basically zombies," she told me.

Good to know.

Using my gun, I shot the lock off the door and then pulled out the chain. Once it was free, Liv and I knelt down and yanked the storm doors open. The musty smell of urine and stale air hit me and I gagged.

Liv peered into the darkness and then at me.

"Ready?"

I nodded.

Wrinkling my nose, I stepped into the dimly lit stairwell and walked downward. After about ten steps we reached a dusty, earth-packed floor. A flickering torch sat on the wall, illuminating a giant open room…

My throat tightened with emotion at the sight of over a hundred women and children.

One of them held a stone in her hand and was at least six months pregnant. She looked ready to crack me over the skull with it. She stood protectively in front of a younger girl who looked like her, about six years old. They both had dusty brown hair and wide green eyes.

"We're not here to hurt you. We came to free you," I choked out, holding my palms flat in a pose of submission.

"Those were the ones who rode the dragon!" someone hissed.

So they had seen us last time. That was good.

Liv stepped up next to me, her eyes glistening with tears. "We're … your children. We were sold to the hunter society."

The woman holding the stone dropped it with a thwack and then lurched forward, sobbing as she crashed into Liv. She wrapped her arms around Liv and the two hugged as other women pushed forward to touch Liv and me. They grasped my arms, my hair, my legs in affectionate strokes. Murmurs rose up among the others at Liv's declaration.

"One of ours?"

"We're saved."

"One of our daughters?"

"Sold to the evil lady!"

They all whispered and spoke quickly, I couldn't track the voices and my own emotions were hard to get into check. My chest heaved as I forced down a sob.

The crowd of women and children parted, kicking up dust as shafts of filtered light shone on the same Asian woman I'd recognized. She stepped forward with a slight limp, tears streaming down her face, making tracks in the dust. She was holding the hand of the little teenage girl I noticed from before.

"Are you … Aspen?" she croaked. "Because … I think you're mine."

You're mine. Her words nearly brought me to my knees.

All I could do was nod as my tears rapidly blurred my vision. The next second I was pulled into a hug and her embrace was everything I thought it would be.

Safe.

Home.

Mother.

I sobbed and she held me even harder. "I tried to keep you," she said, "They took my big toe for trying to run." I pulled back then and looked down at her left foot. Sure enough, it was missing her big toe. The skin was white and thick, a-long-time-ago scar that was jagged and poorly healed. That must be why she limped. "I'm so sorry." Her voice broke.

My heart ripped open. She'd clearly held this guilt within her all along, and I didn't want her to. It wasn't her fault.

I shook my head, reaching for her hand. "It's okay. I understand."

My gaze flicked to the girl who stood near the woman … my mother.

"Aspen, this is Maple. She's your half-sister," my mom stated. We'd clearly both been named after trees and that made me smile. For the first time, I'd learned something about my name.

"Hey." Maple gave me a nervous wave and I smiled.

"Hey."

Despite the fact that we were in the middle of a

freaking war, I'd just discovered my family, and it meant everything to me.

My mom leaned into my ear and whispered. "They let us keep one child eventually, so that they can force us to keep making more without complaint. Maple will be the next breeder now that I've gone through menopause. It keeps the cycle going forever."

"No," I growled, the horror of what she'd just told me igniting my anger in new ways. "We're getting all of you out of here. Now!"

She looked fearfully at me, peering up the stairs and following the sounds of bloodshed outside. Wolves snarled, swords clanged, guns discharged.

"Every single person is going out today!" I shouted to the women as more poured from the basement, which seemed to run across the entire span of the fort.

"They're powerful!" a woman screamed. "The Munai will kill us all and take our children!"

I looked over at Liv, who was speaking to a woman in hushed tones. Liv was crying and I wondered if that was her mom. She didn't look like her. The blond hair and fair skin didn't fit, but maybe she got her coloring from her dad.

"We've brought over a hundred vampires and werewolves with us. They're up there right now carving a pathway out of here for us. Be ready to move in five minutes!" I barked the order and the women stared at me, stunned.

Liv stepped forward. "You heard her! Gather your things. We leave today. You're all getting freed! *Now!*"

I guess it took those words to make them move, because they burst into a flurry of activity. I told my mom and half-sister to get any possessions they could not live without and they nodded, running back into a tunnel that branched out from the main open area. This place was more dungeon than basement.

How long had they been kept down here? In the dark, peeing in buckets and God knows what. It was horrifying.

Liv walked over to me, wiping tears from her eyes, and I froze. "What happened? Was that … your mom?"

Liv shook he head. "She knew my mom. Said I looked just like her. My mom was killed a few weeks after I was born. She went ballistic and attacked the Munai."

Silence and heaviness hung in the air between us; my throat tightened with unshed tears. "Oh, Livvie. I'm so sorry." I pulled her into a hug, wrapping my arms around her. "She was a warrior, just like you."

She laughed, mixed with a sob, and nodded as I pulled away. We both wiped our eyes, and I wasn't sure what to say now. I'd met my mom, and hers was gone, and I somehow felt guilty for that.

After fully drying her eyes once more, she nodded, putting on her game face. Her jaw clenched and eyes turned into a glare. "Let's get everyone out. We can honor her that way."

"Of course," I told her. I hadn't really even thought that either of our moms would still be here and alive and now I was unprepared for mine to be here and not hers.

'Hey. I've got all the women and children almost ready to go. How is it looking up there?' I asked Luka.

He didn't respond at first, which made me nervous, but finally his voice broke through.

'Not ideal. There are more of them than we thought. They were totally expecting us. Have the women be ready to run. I have a plan that requires a quick exit.'

Did I even want to know what that entailed? I guess I would see.

"Be ready to run! Grab your things. Pick up the children," I ordered. I heard clanking noises as the women hurried forward, and realized most of them were shackled at the feet. Anger rushed through me. *'Most of the women are shackled at the feet.'*

If his plan involved them running, that wasn't happening.

Luka's rage filtered through our bond. *'Sending Marmal,'* was all he replied.

Grunts and growls came from the doors at the top of the stairs. I walked halfway up and peeked out.

Whoa.

Sage and Demi stood in front of the open cellar, fighting Munai left and right. How were there so many of them? More must have shown up. There was a wolf next to Demi that I guessed was Sawyer, but it was smaller and more feminine looking. It moved as she moved, and as I watched them fight the realization hit me. It was *her* wolf. Split shifter.

Crazy.

The troll who commanded Pearl suddenly sped across the space and slipped behind Sage and Demi, zooming into view.

"Hey, you got a lock problem?" she asked me.

I just nodded, trying to peer past the pandemonium and get a glimpse of Luka. He was nowhere to be seen. It was a bloodbath, and from the looks of it, we'd lost many.

Marmal took the stairs two at a time, but when she came face to face with all of the women and children, her expression sobered.

"If you are shackled, please step forward." Marmal's voice had an urgency to it.

One by one, *clank clank clank*, the women stepped forward, and I realized they were all pregnant. They bound the pregnant ones so they couldn't flee with their merchandise; the others were kept here out of fear for their living child. Whoever masterminded this knew how to manipulate, and it made me sick.

Marmal took in a deep breath and then snapped her fingers once. Suddenly all of the metal cuffs sprang open and fell from their ankles, clattering to the floor. There were gasps, open weeping, and looks of wonder as Marmal's cheeks went red.

Okay … so *that's* what troll magic did.

"We need to go. Many are dying," Marmal told me.

I nodded.

"Get ready to run," I announced to everyone present.

My mother and half-sister gathered a small cloth bundle and held hands, stepping up beside me expectantly. I wasn't used to having people to take care of—other than Liv. This would take some time.

'Coming out. Ready?' I asked Luka.

'Yes,' he said, but I felt fear take hold of him and filter into me. What kind of plan was this?

I led the women up the steps and out into the

melee, just in time to see Luka appear in the center of the pandemonium. He was covered in black and red blood; it mixed down his arms in a gory show of death and war.

He took a deep breath and then threw his arms out, looking at everyone present. "I command that you *stand down!*"

Power lashed out of his voice as if it were a physical *thing* and knocked into my chest with such force it took my breath away.

Everyone stopped. They just froze what they were doing, and Luka started to shake, gritting his teeth.

It hit me then, what he was doing.

Dominus coercere. Master of compulsion. Instead of focusing on one person like a normal sane man would do, he'd compulsed all of them!

"Run!" I told the women, knowing that this was what he meant. He couldn't hold them off forever, but for now he'd literally paused the war so that they could escape. These women didn't need to be told twice. The second I issued the command and stepped out of the way, they started to flee toward the open gates.

I passed a frozen Demi and Sage, though Demi was starting to move as if wading through water or sand. I think Luka didn't have as good of aim for his gift as he'd thought and he'd frozen most of our people too, but luckily the women and I were free.

The little children slipped from their mothers' grasps, falling to the floor, and the women yanked them into their arms. They looked around in wonder at the frozen fey, Munai, vampires, and wolves. I had no idea Luka had this kind of power.

I waited until the last woman was free of the fort before I stepped into the back of the line and followed them out. When I looked back over my shoulder, at Luka, my heart sank into my stomach. A thin rivulet of blood ran down his nose and ears, and his body shook violently.

"Luka!" I shouted, spinning away from the line of fleeing women and back to my man.

"GO!" he yelled, and that power slapped into me again. Suddenly I was running for the door against my own will.

I knew then that Luka had the power all along to use compulsion on me but he never did. By the time my feet had carried me outside of the fort, Liv was already leading the women over the hill and hopefully into the empty buss. Luka's power suddenly fell away from me then and I turned around. A scream ripped from my throat just as Luka hit the ground and the fighting continued.

"Luka!" I wailed, running back into the fort now

that the spell over me had been lifted. I pulled my katanas, mowing down fey left and right, as I beelined it for Luka.

Sawyer heard my distress and followed my gaze to see his best friend crumpled on the ground. He put his fingers between his lips, whistling loud. "Retreat!"

I reached Luka just in time for a Munai to advance on him.

"Not today, demon!" I pulled my Glock and unloaded two rounds into her head, before I sliced through her neck with ease and her head hit the ground with a thump.

I pulled Luka over my shoulder, struggling to get his dead weight onto my back.

Everyone was fleeing for the busses, when the shadow passed over my head.

I looked up and relief ran through me.

Pearl.

"Get him out of here!" Demi shouted to me, and indicated to the dragon. When I looked at the alpha, my eyebrows shot upward. She was sticking some type of explosive to the walls of the fort. They looked crudely made, but highly effective if that was C4, which it appeared to be from here.

Marmal ran along the side of the fight, weaving in and out of vampires and wolves tossing fey left and right. Had they had a second contingent show up? There were so many of them.

Pearl landed before me with a thud, shaking the ground as she shook herself. Marmal wasted no time grabbing Luka's ankles and helping me hoist him onto Pearl's back.

"Thanks," I muttered, heaving him onto the dragon and climbing up myself.

"Retreat!" Sawyer called again, and gunshots rang out.

Demi had gotten hold of a shotgun and was pushing the fey into the back portion of the fort, against the wall she'd just rigged the explosives. This gave her men and Luka's time to flood out of the fort and into the open valley.

Pearl kicked off the ground and I steadied myself, hovering over Luka's body to pin him to her back. He wasn't breathing, which would normally alarm the shit out of me, but he was a vampire, so I tried to relax.

'*Wake up*,' I begged, shaking his shoulders and trying to use our bond to sense his consciousness. I was distracted with everything happening around me. My gaze was constantly searching the field below for Liv, my mom, Sage, Demi, and everyone. I didn't want to leave them without help, but Luka was my main priority now. The only comfort I had in Luka's health was that his body hadn't turned to ash yet. That meant he was still alive.

"Luka!" I sobbed, slapping his face lightly. He was so pale, cold and unmoving. He looked dead … which, technically, he was, but he didn't look like normal Luka, and I was starting to lose it. A sob ripped from my throat as I clutched his shirt, helpless to do anything. You couldn't exactly give CPR to a dead person.

Marmal looked back at me, compassion pulling at her troll features, causing the tusks in her cheeks to dip downward.

She flew Pearl low to the ground so that we could help if needed, but it looked like Demi and Sawyer had everything handled. The Paladin wolves now had their bowmen shooting arrows to keep the fey and Munai inside of the fort while the last few vampires fled. Demi stood behind the line of Paladin warriors and pulled a black plastic remote out of her pocket.

Boom time.

A second after I had that thought, the C4 went off, sending an explosive mushroom cloud up into the atmosphere. A shockwave blew outward, sending dust and debris into the open field, and my eardrums shook with the force of the blow. Demi and her men retreated toward the busses.

As the cloud of smoke thinned, I saw the walls of the structure had completely collapsed. It was now just a pile of debris with no movement.

Whoa.

We did it.

We won.

I sagged forward, laying on Luka's chest and relaxing my nerves.

Luka groaned then and I bolted upright, hovering over his face as my long red hair made a curtain around us.

His eyes were having trouble focusing as he reached up to touch my hair. "Is this heaven?" he asked.

I grinned, sighing in relief. "You scared me."

He'd told me that compulsion had its consequences, but I hadn't known almost dying was one of them.

He rolled onto his side and then sat up, straddling Pearl and holding on to my thighs to steady himself. Peering over the side, he looked at the three busses that were now retreating.

"Your mom get out?"

I nodded. "And half-sister and everyone else."

He let out a whoop and pulled me in for a kiss, but I turned my head, giving him my cheek.

"Damn your morals, woman! I haven't touched Cassara. I belong to *you*," he growled.

I belong to you. Four of the sexiest words I'd ever heard him say.

"You're married," I pressed.

Marmal raised an eyebrow, but said nothing. How embarrassing, she probably thought I was his mistress. I guess I kind of was, as much as I'd tried to avoid that.

"For now. But not for much longer," he promised.

That was too vague for me. I wanted to throat punch him, but he'd probably fall off and break his neck.

I sighed, feeling fully depressed by the situation.

He pulled my chin up and forced me to look him in the eyes. "I haven't touched her. I want you to know that."

I raised one eyebrow. Yeah, right. They'd been married for days. I doubted Cassara would allow that.

"You mean you never?" I raised one eyebrow, finding it too hard to believe. She seemed like an adamant woman, and if he had slept with her, I couldn't fault him. They *were* married.

He shook his head. "Nope. And she's pissed. I'll dissolve the marriage based on the grounds we haven't consummated."

I couldn't believe we were having this conversation while riding on a freaking dragon! His nonchalant attitude at annulling his marriage shocked me.

"But then you can't be king without a wife and heirs." Did he truly know what he was saying?

He ran his fingers through his hair. "You let me worry about that, okay? Just trust me."

Alright. He'd earned that much, hadn't he?

Leaning into him, I snuggled in close. His arms wrapped around me.

If we could just stay like this, flying high above the city without ever having to return to reality, that would be great.

But, unfortunately, I knew that wasn't an option.

BETWEEN LUKA, Demi, and Sawyer, they'd split all of the breeder survivors into three even groups and offered to take in one group each. Of course, my mother and half-sister were in the group that now lived in Vampire City. The survivors were given accommodations in the more modern portion of Vampire City where the feeders lived. It was thought they would be among humans and feel the most normal there.

The fey didn't try to retaliate after our invasion. Luka had evidence of their crimes in the spoken testimony of the freed women if they ever tried. Besides, the werewolf-vampire alliance was too strong. So long as the vampires and werewolves stood together, the fey wouldn't try anything. All the more reason for Luka to remain king.

My mom and Maple were allowed to live in the

guest house with me and Liv. We all had fun getting to know each other over the next two days. It was traumatic at times. One of us would ask a question that clearly triggered trauma, and then we had to gracefully change the subject, but all in all my mom and Maple seemed settled. They were just glad to be free.

"So will you go back to hunting in Spokane, or stay here?" my mom wondered aloud at dinner. I'd told her all about Maz and her lies, but also that I did like my job of protecting the humans and that I wanted to eventually continue to do that.

"I dunno. I'd love to have my own hunter guild or something," I told her honestly.

"Ohhhh, hunter guild. Cool name." Liv shoved a piece of potato into her mouth and I chuckled.

"I want to be a hunter!" Maple said, gripping her butterknife like it was a stake.

"No," my mom and I both said at the same time, and then the entire table erupted into laughter. Well, everyone but Maple.

"You suck." She crossed her arms and glared at us both.

Somehow, I thought the teenage drama and angst would pass over her since she was raised without TV or any pop culture references, but I was wrong. She was as feisty as ever.

"It's dangerous. Maybe when you're older," I amended.

My mom cut me a playful glare. "Or maybe *never*. I can't have both of my babies risking their life every day."

My babies.

My mom did that a lot. She just threw endearing words and pet names out there like she had already accepted me and loved me and time hadn't passed between us. It was the best damn feeling in the world. But I knew it sliced a hole into Liv's heart. Liv's entire body tensed when my mom did that stuff; her eyes grew vacant. We'd both grown up together as orphans. We had no lovey-dovey mom, just a strong mentor like Maz, who turned out to be a psycho. I knew Liv was seeking that connection that I now had with my mom and I felt awful about it.

Reaching out, I squeezed Liv's hand and a single tear rolled down her cheek. The table quieted and my mom leaned over to Maple. "Honey, go watch some TV for a bit, okay?"

Maple nodded, all too eager to watch her new favorite device, and left the table.

"I'm fine." Liv waved my hand off and shoved a spoonful of rice into her mouth, more tears streaming down her face.

My mom stood, walked over to Liv's side of the table and pulled the spoon out of her hand, placing it on her plate.

"Look at me," my mom ordered her. I was shocked at the strength left in a woman who had been beaten into submission for so long.

Liv looked up at my mom, who dropped to her knees before my bestie. Tears streamed down Liv's face as she could no longer hold her feelings in.

"I want to tell you a story." My mom smiled. "I was at your birth."

Liv stilled, her mouth popping open. She wiped her tears quickly, perking up.

"I was a new mother myself, but I'd been selected to become a midwife at the encampment, so I was to learn from your mother's delivery as part of my training."

I leaned closer to Liv, wanting to hear every word of this story as well.

"Most of us were born into the encampment for generations. My mother was a breeder, and her mother, and so on. When we go through menopause, if we are not of use in another way … we're disposed of."

My heart squeezed. She'd lived in slavery her entire life? I couldn't conceive of it.

"Your mother, Genevieve, was not born into the

camp," my mom said. "She was stolen. Brought in from the human world. She taught us many things about the outside world. She was a camp favorite." I could see the tears welling in my own mother's eyes as she went down memory lane.

Liv reached out and grasped my mom's hand.

"Her birth was long and laborious, but when I set you in her arms, something about her changed in that moment. It changes for all of us…" She smiled at me. "But with her, she didn't have the resignation we all have, knowing we will be forced to give our children up." My mom's voice cracked as she looked at me for a moment. "A fire was lit under your mother that day. I saw the moment it happened. It was the moment she looked at you. She intended to get out with you and raise you herself."

Liv burst into sobs then, her head hanging forward. My mom reached out and pulled Liv in for a hug and the two of them held each other for a long few moments. Finally, Liv pulled back and wiped her eyes. "What happened?"

My mom sighed. "Are you sure you want to hear the rest?"

Liv nodded, a hardness coming over her face. "Hold nothing back."

"Very well." My mom wiped her own eyes. "Genevieve asked a few of us to help her escape. You were only a few weeks old and she was barely healed. We agreed. One night, as the guards were changing shift, she placed you on her breast for feeding in order to keep you quiet."

I could barely breathe, I was so enthralled in the story.

"I went out into the courtyard screaming and holding my belly, pretending to be injured." My mother's face took on a haunted look as if she didn't want to relive that night but would for Liv's sake. "The guards rushed to me, and that's when your mom slipped out and made her run for it."

She was quiet for a full minute and I wasn't sure she was going to finish. It was too painful. I could see that now.

"You don't have to—" Liv started, but my mom waved her off.

"The Munai caught her at the gate, and your mom's scream ripped through the entire encampment. I could just see from my place on the ground, the moonlight showing me what transpired." My mom nodded to herself. "Normally, if we try to run, they take a toe or cut out our tongue, but your mother killed a Munai. She went insane. I've never seen a woman so strong, with so much anger and determination. It was the most beautiful rebellion I'd ever witnessed."

I lost sight of the room then, because tears filled my eyes so strongly that everything blurred.

"The guards left me, and took you before killing your mother right then and there."

I blinked rapidly to clear the tears, and Liv nodded, reaching out to clasp my mom's hands. "Thank you for that," Liv whimpered. "It meant everything for me to hear her story."

My mom bobbed her head. "They let us name our kids. It's the one thing they give us. She named you after Olivia Newton John. She was a huge fan of some movie called *Grease*, I guess?"

Liv and I both burst into crying laughter then, and my mom's face brightened.

"You know the movie?" my mom asked.

Liv nodded. "I mean it's older, but I've seen it. Wow. That's funny and cool. Thank you again."

She reached out and hugged my mom for the umpteenth time. When my mom pulled back, she brushed her hands over Liv's curly hair. "Aspen tells me you're like sisters, so as far as I'm concerned, that makes you mine … if you want."

Holy moly, the tears were just coming left and right. I'd only known this woman a few days and already I was gobsmacked at the amount of compassion and strength she possessed. Liv just nodded, unable to speak, and my mom grinned ear to ear.

"Lucky me," my mom said, but I was pretty sure it was lucky us.

We finished our dinner and then went into the living room with Maple and decided to watch *Grease*. We smiled and laughed and it brought such a lightness to the house. It felt like Liv's mom was right here with us, looking down with joy.

"I'm totally calling you Olivia now," I teased as the credits to the movie rolled. I stood up and stretched. It was late and I was exhausted.

"Don't you dare. No disrespect to my mom, but I'm Liv," she pressed.

We all laughed and my mom had to drag my sleepy sis away from the TV she was obsessed with, and pull her down the hall to bed.

"Night!" I told everyone as they wished me a goodnight as well. Luka had come by this morning for a feeding so I wasn't going to see him until tomorrow. I hated this time apart. He'd been married to Cassara about a week now, a week too long in my opinion. But as he asked, I'd chosen to trust him.

I brushed my teeth and then slipped into my room. As I was just tucking under the covers, my burner phone rang.

My eyes snapped open and I scrambled upright, launching across the room to the dresser where I kept it plugged in. I'd carried this thing around with me everywhere for days and it had finally rung!

I pulled it open and pressed it to my ear. "Hello?"

Ruby's voice came across the line: "Do you want answers?"

Yes, I wanted answers, but I didn't know who to trust.

"How did you get this number?" I asked her.

"Sterling," she responded, and my whole body froze. He'd contacted Ruby before he died? Why?

"Tell me about Ma—" I started, but she cut me off.

"If you want answers, meet me at the place you and Sterling first kissed. He told me where it was and that it would be a sign to trust me. Be there at eight a.m., otherwise I'm writing you off as an ally."

The line went dead.

I stared at the phone in my hand in shock, her words rushing through me.

Sterling told her about our first kiss in Manito Park? Then he must have wanted me to trust her. The very least I could do would be to honor his name by meeting with her.

I rushed into Liv's room and told her everything, relaying every word while it was still fresh in my mind.

"You think Sterling found a connection with

Ruby or something and spoke to her before he died?" she asked.

"I don't know, but only you, me, Sterling, and Vasquez know we had our first kiss in Manito Park. If she's there, it's because Sterling told her and we should trust her."

Liv chewed her lip. "Things were just settling down here."

"Liv! Don't you want answers? Don't you want to make Maz pay for what she's done?"

A hardened expression came over my bestie. "Absolutely. We'll leave at first light."

Relief and trepidation wormed through me. This was what I wanted for so long, but Liv was right. We'd freed my mom and the others, there was peace for a moment, and I kind of wanted to just soak in that while I could catch my breath.

But God had other plans.

"No. Nope. Not a chance in hell." Luka crossed his arms and glared at me. We stood beside the dining table in Liv and I's cottage. I'd actually grown to love this little house. Luka's lips were tinged red from feeding. I'd been waiting until after to tell him Liv and I were leaving this morning.

"Umm, I wasn't asking." *That was awkward.* "I was telling you. I'll be back in two days, tops. I won't let you starve." I winked.

Luka's face fell. "This isn't about me starving. I'm worried about you getting hurt."

"Because then you'll starve?" Where was my anger coming from? Oh yeah, he'd been married to Cassara over a week and was *still* married to the wench. Even after promising me an annulment.

His face fell. "You have no idea how much I care about you…"

His words sobered me, dousing my anger.

"And I guess that's my fault. Aspen, please don't go." He reached out and pulled me into him, cradling my head under his chin.

God, I loved being held by him. It was so safe.

"My mom and Maple will stay and pose as your feeders. I'll be back in less than forty-eight hours." I had to go. I had to get the answers I sought.

He pulled back and grasped my chin, looking down at me. "I'll send a guard of—"

"No. She said to come alone. I can't spook her. Luka, I'm a hunter. I'll be fine."

Luka growled, "You can't expect me to let you go alone!"

"I'm going with Liv," I deadpanned.

"You know what I mean," he said through clenched teeth.

Anger flared up inside of me. "I'm not your wife, Luka. You can't tell me what to do and then go home to her!" I shouted and spun, storming away from him.

I threw the door open wide and the look on Liv's face told me she'd heard everything. Shame burned through me. Luka had been nothing but nice to us, taking us in when we had no money and nowhere to go. But it felt at this point like he was toying with me. Promising me he'd leave Cassara and then doing nothing.

'I'm sorry,' I sent through our bond. But he didn't respond.

Great. The one person I was bound to forever was mad at me.

MANITO PARK HAD a plethora of gardens, including a Japanese garden and a rose garden. The rose garden portion of it was where Sterling and I had our first kiss. I parked my Bug, stepping out and stretching my back. It was about an hour and fifteen minutes from Vampire City to here. I pulled my jacket over the Glock at my hip, concealing it, as Liv tucked a dagger into her boot. I had no idea if this was a trap or not, but we owed it to Sterling and all of the hunters to try to get to the bottom of this.

"Sterling wouldn't tell her where we kissed unless he trusted her," I told Liv.

Liv didn't look so sure. "Unless Ruby is the one who killed Sterling and got that out of him before she took his head."

My stomach sank. She was right. We couldn't be sure. "I'll meet her alone, you slip into the trees. If there is a struggle you come up behind her."

Liv nodded, disappearing into the park and then the woods beyond. I let out a shaky breath. We'd gotten up so early in order to get ready and feed Luka before the long drive, I hadn't had time to have caffeine, something I was now regretting.

After locking my car, I headed into the park. There were a few people out and about, mostly on walks or biking the trails. One loved-up couple was having a breakfast picnic on a blanket. I crossed the open grass area and went around the building that concealed the rose park. This time of year they would all be in bloom. Striding up the steps, I looked out onto the pinks and reds and golds of the buds and petals and in that moment I remembered Sterling. We hadn't even had a burial for him…

Guilt ate away at me until I heard Ruby's voice. "Aspen."

I jumped a little, spinning with my hand tucked under my jacket and on the trigger of my weapon.

She was alone, but she was also packing heat, hand on her blade. We both looked at each other for a moment, sizing the other up.

I could tell she didn't know whether or not to trust me, which made me trust her in that moment. I decided to go first. "I raided the breeder camp in Magic City three days ago and freed my biological mom. The women there have babies that psycho

Maz buys and then sells to the Vampire Hunter Society."

Ruby sighed, pulling her hand away from her weapon and extending her arms to hug me. She pulled me into her and I allowed it, wrapping my arms around her. My idol. Ruby Thorn.

"I knew you were a good kid when I met you in Portland. It's so hard to know who to trust right now," she murmured against my ear.

I pulled back and she looked out into the tree line, waving. Another hunter stepped out into the morning light and I chuckled.

"Your backup?"

She nodded.

I waved into the woods beyond her and Liv stepped out, causing Ruby to grin.

"Let's sit and talk. It goes so much deeper than you think."

After we settled into an unpopulated portion of the park, Ruby rubbed her forehead in a sign of stress. "I was on to Maz since last year. I didn't know what exactly was wrong, but as I made it higher up into the ranks of the society, I started to see things that didn't make sense. Only Maz got the files from our connection at the chief of police, only Maz brought in babies from the orphanage, Maz held all the money … you get the idea."

I nodded, swallowing hard as Liv leaned in closer.

Ruby looked at me honestly. "I… I don't even know where to begin."

I shrugged. "Sterling?"

She swallowed hard. "I'm sorry to hear about what happened to him. They're saying he fell in the line of duty. Maz had a whole vigil for him and everything."

Anger flared up inside of me at that. Fell in battle!

"That's bullshit," Liv seethed.

Ruby nodded, her long braid shaking at her back. "I know. Sterling contacted me and said he wanted to meet up. I thought it odd a House of Rose hunter would want to meet with me, but he was acting paranoid and urgent over the phone, speaking in code and such, so I figured I would meet him and see what this was about."

She continued: "We met up at Gonzaga University campus. He said he was going to meet you right after at Riverfront … I feel awful that—"

I reached out and grasped her shoulder. "It's not your fault." My throat was tight.

Gonzaga was right by Riverfront. It meant that Maz had gotten to Sterling directly after his meeting with Ruby and right before he was going to meet me. He'd probably only been dead minutes before I saw his head in that box. Maz had clearly followed him and waited for the perfect time to strike. I just wondered if she'd seen him with Ruby and if her life was in danger now.

If only I'd come sooner, drove faster, ran instead of walked … maybe I could have intercepted.

I pushed all the guilt away. "What did you guys talk about?"

Ruby nodded. "As much as we could in ten minutes' time. I told him what I knew, that I thought the orphans coming into the society were stolen, or bought, and he told me about them not even being fully human. That none of us are."

I bobbed my head in understanding and she continued.

"I also told him I'd found evidence that the marks we kill don't have genuine crimes in their files, that a Chief Baker exists but he has nothing to do with the society unless he's really good and hiding his ties to us."

"I knew it!" Liv hissed.

"We found the breeder farm," I reminded Ruby. "I actually found my mom. We freed them all, so you don't need to worry about that anymore."

Ruby shared a look with her fellow hunter, a tall male about twenty years old. It was a sketchy look.

"What?" I asked. Feeling like a bomb was about to drop.

Ruby cleared her throat. "After Sterling died, I did some digging. I've had to be careful, because I assume Maz knows I met with Sterling that day if she followed him."

I licked my lips nervously. "And?"

"You know how there are hunter societies all over the place? Chicago, New York, New Orleans, Los Angeles…?"

I nodded. "Yeah…" Not to mention the international ones.

Ruby chewed on her bottom lip. "Aspen, in each of those cities there is a magical enclave of hidden supernaturals. And within that, there is a breeder program with orphans that are bought to supply the system with hunters … assassins."

The edges of the park blurred then as dizziness washed over me. "Wait, what?"

But it made sense, right? I knew there were hunters all over because there were vampires and witches and werewolves all over that needed hunting … I just assumed they all came from the Magic City enclave in Idaho.

"How many?" My voice shook.

Ruby pulled out a small piece of paper. Words had been scratched out and rewritten and lines connected to other words; there was even a crudely drawn map. "So far, I have confirmed six breeder programs in the US throughout the various hidden magical enclaves."

I was too shocked to say anything.

Six. Six slave encampments like the one that my mom was in. It made me sick to my stomach.

"How can you even find that out? They are so secretive, we barely found ours, and only because we knew someone who had heard about them."

Ruby glanced to the dude with her and he cleared his throat. "Sterling tipped us off to the purchases, and from there it was easy. There's a lot of dates, but I was able to follow the money trail and see whenever Maz wired a certain amount. In our day, it was ten thousand. Now it's fifty."

"Fifty grand for a baby. That's sick!" I jumped up, feeling bile rise in my throat. "She's a demon, she's the fucking devil as far as I'm concerned. We have to kill her!"

Ruby stood and met me head on, a fierceness flashing in her eyes. "We will. Trust me, no one wants that more than you and I, but there are other players involved. She doesn't do this alone. Fiona in New York, and Alonzo in Chicago, to name a few. We need to map out all the ringleaders and take them all out at once. Otherwise, they will rebuild once we kill Maz."

I tipped my head back and screamed in frustration, causing a few passersby to glance at me worriedly.

"Hey…" Ruby reached out and grasped my shoulders. "We can do this. If we put all of our resources together, we can stop them all."

"Maz drained our bank accounts, we have no money," I said.

Ruby nodded. "I'm probably going to be cut off next. I've been transferring money to another bank and pulling out cash weekly. I'm not talking about money though, Aspen … you have other assets at your disposal."

I frowned, confused.

"Sterling told me you had … a connection with the vampires. That you had a way inside Magic City. That much is clear if you've already broken up one breeder program there."

Oh, that. Luka.

"I do," I told her, "The vampire king and I are … close."

She waved me off. "You don't need to explain. I don't judge anything anymore. It's all been a lie."

I nodded. "What do you need?"

Ruby handed me the paper she'd scribbled on. "I

need the exact locations of the breeder programs inside these enclaves so we can take them all down together. Our clock may have just moved up since you've already taken one out. Word will spread."

I frowned. "You think they all talk?"

Ruby again shared a look with her hunter companion. "Aspen, each enclave produces five million dollars in babies a year. Times six, that's a thirty-million-dollar-a-year industry for the dark fey."

Shit.

And it then supplied hunters who would take out the vampires and werewolves in the outside world. The big bad that could stand up against the fey. And they took a cut of our bounty fee. The real numbers could be much higher.

"Wait…" It dawned on me. "That's why they do it. The fey supply endless hunters to Maz to control the vampire population."

Ruby nodded. "Yep, and better yet, Maz is one hundred percent dark fey."

She pulled a folder out of her bag and handed to me. Her revelation sent chills up my spine. I couldn't process them. But I remembered being stumped at the fact that she never really seemed to age.

Opening the folder, I gasped when I saw various pictures of Maz. Most were black and white and she was wearing eighteenth-century clothing. She looked the same age as now, about fifty or sixty.

"We think Maz is a Munai. A high priestess fey," Ruby shared. "She's basically going to live forever until killed, and has the power to charm her look to appear human."

I dropped the photos back into the folder as my mouth hung open. Glancing at Liv, I noticed she looked as blindsided as me.

Maz … a Munai?

"But … I don't understand." The Munai were horrible, evil, black-net belching psychos.

Ruby leaned in closely. "Understand this. No one over thirty years old remains in the Vampire Hunter Society. They ask too many questions, and one of which is probably why Maz doesn't appear to age. I'm lucky to still be alive, though I won't be for long unless I run too."

Maz adopted and paid for the babies, and then turned them into little God-fearing warriors who would do her bidding without question. All while controlling the vampire problem, the one race that could take over the fey if they got too powerful. Hadn't Luka said it himself? The vampires and were-wolves together were unbeatable.

"Where will you go?" I asked.

Ruby looked out onto the park. "I can't leave my

hunters. I'll either have to tell my whole team or let Maz come for me."

My heart ached at her loyalty. She wouldn't leave her hunters to be brainwashed. That was a true leader.

"Gather your hunters. Tell them everything, and then bring them to the Magic City enclave in Idaho. You can all stay in Vampire City while we plan our attack and bring the entire society to its knees."

Ruby raised an eyebrow. "Fifty hunters and a dozen orphans are going to be warmly accepted into Vampire City? Says who?"

I sighed. "The vampire king."

Liv was giving me a wide eyed maybe-you-should-talk-to-Luka-first look, but I didn't care. I was doing this, now or never. If Maz took out Ruby, then it would be all the harder for me to take on the society as a whole by myself.

"If you can promise us a safe place to stay, I will evacuate the entire House of Thorns," Ruby promised.

'Luka,' I pressed into his mind. *I know you're mad at me for leaving this morning, but quick question, can fifty vampire hunters and a dozen orphans come stay in Vampire City? They are fleeing from Maz.'

I felt him bristle at my question through our bond.

'*Please,*' I added. '*They're in trouble.*'

'*I would never deny you anything,*' came his reply, and my cheeks heated at that.

"You can come. The vampire king will protect you," was all I said.

Ruby looked to her companion and he nodded.

"Very well. Be ready for us in a few days. I'll call you on the same number to coordinate everything." She smoothed her braid and looked out at the tree line.

"What?" I asked her. A somber mood had fallen over our little group, but I sensed she had more to say.

"I was never into the religious aspect of being a hunter, which is why I chose House of Thorn, but … I bought Maz's sales pitch that the vampires were evil murdering rapists with no self-control. I've killed so many…" Her eyes grew distant; the guilt was eating at her as it did to me.

"We all believed it, and no doubt some deserved it. We just have to move forward now with what we do know." I grasped her hand. She nodded, rapidly blinking away tears.

"Thank you, Aspen. I wasn't sure where to go from here, but I think together we can change things. Forever." She reached over and gave me a hug.

I wrapped my arms around her and squeezed, pulling back to look her in the eyes. "When it's time to take Maz down, I want to be the one," I told her through clenched teeth.

Surprise mixed with pride shone on her face, and she nodded once.

I wanted Maz to look down the barrel of a shotgun while I pulled the trigger and then took her head off with razor wire.

"I'll call you." Ruby stood and gave us both a subtle nod before leaving. Liv and I sat there for a long while just watching the people meander in and out of the rose garden.

"Tons more breeder enclaves," Liv said somberly.

I nodded. "I can't even imagine…"

"We have to stop them all," she declared. "For my mom. For yours. For all of the women."

I inclined my head, reaching out to squeeze her hand. "We will. We totally will."

Liv looked over at me. "Do you think Maz gave Sterling a hunter's burial? I mean, if she had a service for him…"

My heart suddenly felt like it had grown wings. "Yes! Let's go." I pulled her upright and she smiled as we ran to my car, stopping only once to snap off a single white rose.

If Maz was keeping the illusion of Sterling falling

in battle, she would have buried him in the society cemetery with all of the other fallen hunters. The least I could do while I was here was pay my respects.

It was a short drive to the private society cemetery. I'd been here a couple times in my years growing up around hunters, but the most memorable was when I was fifteen. I'd come for Mia's funeral. She'd fallen in battle—or at least that's what Maz had told us. Now I wondered if she'd just gotten too close, found something out. Mia was one of my fighting instructors and a senior hunter. Her death had hit us all hard.

"Thinking of Mia?" Liv asked as I passed farmland and pulled into the open gates of the graveyard.

I nodded. "It's the day we made our backup plan, remember? Our way out?"

Liv grinned. "Private island and hottie husbands."

I snickered. How naive we were, thinking we could just make enough money and leave. When Maz wanted you gone, you were gone, and now we didn't even have our money. Not that I wanted that dirty blood money now anyway.

"You think Maz knows about the Yaak Montana house?" I asked Liv.

Liv nodded. "We wired the cash from the society's chosen credit union. She probably owns the freaking bank."

That was depressing. I loved that place, and now we really had nowhere to go if shit hit the fan. I guess we had Vampire City, but that didn't feel like home. Not yet. After parking my Beetle off to the side, we roamed the multiple acreage graveyard until finally, in the back right corner by a weeping willow tree, I saw the freshly churned earth in a mound. I walked over hesitantly, Liv following behind me. I was scared to see his name, scared to have the finality of it burned into my soul.

Sterling was dead, I knew that. I saw his head, but this … this made it real.

The closer I got, the easier it was to make out the letters carved into the granite headstone.

Sterling Rose.

It was him.

Sterling was gone.

I fell to my knees before the grave as fresh, hot grief ripped through me. A sob erupted in Liv's throat and she knelt beside me, reaching for my hand.

"He was like a brother to me." She could barely speak around the emotion in her throat.

I nodded. "He was my first love."

Liv put her arm around me and I leaned into her as we both wept softly. The guilt I carried for pulling him into this would probably never leave me, but at least I had the peace of knowing his body lay undisturbed and his soul was with God now.

I wiped my eyes just as a shadow passed over us. Reacting on instinct, I pulled my Glock from under my jacket and spun.

Maz was creeping forward, holding a sword in her left hand and a sleek black gun in her right. Without hesitation, I popped off two shots right into her chest. She squeezed the trigger of her weapon at the same time. Pain sliced into my right upper arm and I was thrown backward with the force of the bullet. Wasting no time, Liv surged forward and kicked the gun out of Maz's hand. It flew off into the grass a few feet away.

Our mentor was on one knee, wincing in pain, but not laid out flat like she should be after getting shot twice in the chest with a Glock 9mm. Blood pooled the front of her priestess robe as she gripped her sword and glared at Liv and I.

Her silver hair and homely face flickered in and out as something more grotesque began to emerge underneath.

Black stringy hair, pointed ears, dark eyes with no color…

Demon.

Munai.

Her charm was slipping. The two bullets I'd shot into her chest fell to the ground. Somehow they had been pushed out and Maz stood, grinning, as she palmed her sword.

Completely healed.

"I knew you would come here. You're too weak and stupid to stay hidden," Maz seethed.

Having a woman who I'd thought of like a grandmother my entire life call me weak and stupid was like a slap to the face.

My gun was still out, Maz's sword was raised, and Liv stood off to the side, hand twitching over the weapon at her hip. We were in a standoff. I was shot in the arm and it wasn't ideal, but I wasn't going to die from it. I should shoot her right between the eyes, but I wasn't sure how much strength I had in my arm after being shot. The gun was getting heavier by the moment, and if I was honest, I wanted some answers.

"You're Munai," I spat.

She raised one eyebrow, a halfcocked grin gracing her face. "Once banished from my community, they now *bow* when I visit. I've built an empire while they sat on their thumbs."

Now it was my turn to grin. "An empire that I tore down in a day."

Fear fickered over her face.

I laughed. "Oh, you haven't heard yet? Your breeder encampment in Magic City has been completely wiped out and all of the women and children are free."

"You lie!" she screamed, and as the guttural roar left her throat, a black smoky blob flew from her mouth.

I pulled the trigger, emptying my clip into the blob, but it did nothing to slow it, and my aim was crap since my arm was going numb. The dark mass slammed into me with the force of a truck. I was thrown back, hitting the ground hard, fully encompassed by this cloud of black smoke. This was different than the black net I'd seen the other Munai shoot out. This was a cloud I couldn't see through, or move through. It was like I'd been thrown in quicksand. In a panic, I struggled to move, but my limbs seized up as if someone were holding me down.

The clang of swords reverberated throughout the cemetery, and I knew Liv was in a fight for her life with Maz.

'What's happening? I feel panic from you,' Luka burst in my thoughts.

Tell him or not tell him? I guess if this is how I was going to die, someone should know.

'I'm stuck in a Munai dark cloud bomb,' I groaned, trying to wiggle free.

'Quick, open the Beetle charm on your bracelet. There is spell-breaking powder in there.'

Charm?

'WHAT! I'm wearing a bracelet with a spell on it!?' I seethed.

'I knew you wouldn't if I told you. Do it, quickly.'

With a growl and great effort, I moved my left arm over to my right wrist and fiddled with the charms.

"Hang on, Liv!" I cried out blindly. Maz was a badass when she was a human. As a Munai I wasn't sure how long my best friend would last against her. The second I felt the round hump of the Beetle charm between my fingers, relief surged through me. Fumbling, I ran my fingers along the bottom and felt for a tiny nub that must have been a button. Pressing the nub, I flipped the bottom of the Beetle charm cap open and prayed for a miracle. A fine dust filled the air in front of me and chased the black smoke away instantly.

Praise God!

With my limbs suddenly free and sight fully restored, I leapt up from the ground. My injured arm was at half capacity, but I was able to quickly insert a new clip into my Glock. Taking in the scene before me, I strode forward with a cry on my lips to where Maz was about to take off Liv's head with her sword. Aiming the gun at the side of Maz's head in an awkward angle that wouldn't shoot Liv, who was knelt in front of the Munai, I pulled the trigger. The explosion rang out and Maz dropped to the ground like a sack of potatoes. Liv dove out of the way and I gave her my hand to pull her up.

"Holy *crap*, that was bad," Liv huffed. "You got shot!"

She was panting, and we both turned to look down at Maz, who was a lifeless heap on the ground.

We'd done it.

Ruby wouldn't be too happy I'd taken down the kingpin of the operation before we could find all the other players, but I'd done what I needed to survive.

You better be alive, woman! And on your way to me,' Luka roared in my head.

"Come on." I pulled Liv away from where Maz's dead body lay. "I need to see a doctor."

Concern crossed Liv's face and she nodded, picking up our weapons and running after me.

'I'm alive,' I told Luka, leaving out the injured part for now. I wanted to get in the car before anyone saw us or Maz's dead body.

"I'll drive!" Liv held out her hands and I tossed her the key, walking faster with each step. My shoulder burned like hell and I was losing feeling in my fingers, which I knew wasn't good. The second we got into the car, I collapsed against the passenger seat and a deep throb started to pulse down my entire back.

"Hey, do we have painkillers? I—" The words died in my throat when a blur in front of the car caught my attention.

Maz … was alive. She'd risen up like a freaking zombie and now ran full speed at our car.

Lord have mercy.

"Go!" I pointed to Maz, and Liv followed my gaze, her eyelids peeling open in shock. Throwing the car into gear, Liv tore out of the lot just as Maz streaked across the cemetery like a zombie on steroids.

"She's alive!" I screeched.

"She's alive." Liv's voice held defeat, horror, fear.

Liv put the pedal to the metal, her gaze flicking to the rearview mirror as my mind chewed over what had just happened.

"That was insane," I breathed.

"Way insane," Liv added.

Maz was a heartless fey who clearly didn't care about God or her "children." She cared about money and power, and I was going to wipe her from the face of this Earth if it was the last thing I did.

But first I needed some medical attention.

Luka's voice came through our bond: *I'm at the border of Magic City. Tell me where you are. Do you need a doctor? Dammit, you should have taken my security detail. I'm never listening to you again!'* Luka was seething mad and I didn't blame him. I almost got killed.

'We are inbound ... I got shot in the arm. But ... it doesn't look too bad.' I winced and prepared for the mental reaming.

It never came. Instead I was met with dead silence.

'Luka?' His silence was actually more powerful than him screaming at me.

'I can't handle you hurt,' was all he said, and my heart softened in that moment. I think I'd been so angry about him still being married to Cassara that I'd built up resentment toward him that was unfounded.

'I'm sorry. Next time I'll take some security. I promise.'

He laughed. *'You're funny if you think I'm ever letting you out of my sight again.'*

And they said werewolves were the most possessive. Not by a long shot.

LUKA JUST STARED down the Ithaki doctor the entire time that he pulled out the bullet in my arm with tweezers and then stitched it up. The doctor had done a nerve block so I wouldn't feel anything and I was able to stay awake for the procedure. He said with my accelerated healing, I should be good to go with full range of motion in my arm in seven days' time. Until then, I needed to lay low or risk reinjuring it and having the tendons heal wrong.

When we were finally alone, Luka looked down at me with a scowl. "You're careless."

My mouth popped open. "I am not! I went in fully armed with Liv at my side, I—"

"No," he growled, leaning closer to me so that I could smell the mint chewing gum on his breath. "You're reckless with my heart."

The shock of his accusation slammed into me, and before I could respond, he spun around and left. He left me alone in the healing ward of the creepy castle.

I didn't know what to say…

You're reckless with my heart.

Had I been? I hadn't meant to … I'd only meant to protect my heart. I sat up and grabbed my things, finding Liv waiting for me in the hallway. She had a few stitches in her arm from where Maz's blade had sliced her, but otherwise we'd walked away pretty lucky from that fight.

"Luka seemed pissed. What happened?" Liv looked down the hallway of the healing ward. Dark stone castles were *not* my vibe.

"I got hurt. I guess he's offended by that," I growled.

Liv nodded. "He's in love with you."

I froze. "No. I mean deep feelings yes, but—"

"He's deeply fucking in love with you, Aspen," Liv said again, and my stomach tied into knots as I let myself hope and believe that could be true.

"He's married," was all I said.

Until he announced his impending divorce, I didn't want to entertain any ideas.

When I got back to the guest cabin, my mom and

Maple fawned over me and inspected my wounds. I didn't exactly tell them what happened, just that it was hunter business gone wrong. The last thing my newly freed mother needed was to hear that there were half a dozen more breeder encampments still in running order. I didn't want her to worry about anything. I wanted her to start a fresh life.

After dinner, I headed off to bed early. The doctor had given me a pain pill and it was hitting me hard now.

The second my head hit the pillow, the pull of sleep called to me, but something kept me conscious for a while.

You're reckless with my heart, played out in my mind over and over until I finally fell asleep.

"WAKE UP, LITTLE BITCH," a female voice purred in my ear.

My eyelids snapped open. Light assaulted my eyes as a hand clamped around my mouth, cutting off my scream. I groaned, looking up at the owner of the voice.

Cassara.

I moved to fight her, even in my impaired and injured state, but a sharp crack sliced into the side of my head and then everything went black.

***

I CAME to with a throbbing headache. Pain pulsed between my eyes, taking away from the pain at my shoulder, and I groaned. My system flooded with panic as the memory of Cassara in my room surfaced. My gaze flicked around the room in terror as I took in the scene before me. My arms were bound behind my back, and I sat in a chair like an interrogation suspect. Cassara stood before me, grinning like a mad fool. There were two other vamp dudes present, one on either side of the door.

Crap.

I was out of my league. No weapons, no hands, injured shoulder, and three vamps.

"You know, I asked my new hubby for *one* thing as my wedding gift," she sneered, and although I was groggy and in pain, I sobered quickly at the hatred in her voice. "I asked him to fire you as his feeder, and do you know what he told me?" Her eyes were wild, blond hair splayed around her head.

"He said *no!*" Cassara yelled, and I flinched at the shrillness. "I don't like being told no." She pulled back her lips to reveal her distended canines.

"Then last night, instead of screwing his brains out, like I should be, he asked me for a divorce!" She reached out and smacked me across the face with her open palm. Fresh stinging pain burst across my cheek and I winced as tears sprang to my eyes.

He asked her for a divorce...

"I know it's because of you," she seethed. "I'm going to put a stop to whatever *thing* you two have. Right. Now." She palmed a twelve-inch hunting blade and my mouth went bone dry. I tried to yanked my arms outward, only to whimper as the pain of the binds tugged on my injured shoulder.

'*Luka, Cassara kidnapped me. Help,*' I pushed through our bond.

'*What! Where are you?*' His reply was instant, panicked, surprised.

I looked around the room. It was made of stone with windows that had stained glass. I relayed the info to him.

'*I'm coming. Tell her you're my bonded feeder, and if she kills you, she kills me and her chance to remain queen of all vampires.*' His voice was rushed and I knew it was because he was probably hauling ass over here. Remain queen? So he would take back the divorce? Or just lead her to believe that?

Cassara pulled the knife up so that it caught the

flicker of light from the bright bulb above us and then lunged for me.

"I'm Luka's bonded feeder! We imprinted!" I yelled just as she slammed the knife into my lower abdomen, all the way up to the hilt. She froze with her hand on the knife as shock marred her face.

Hot searing pain flared to life in my stomach and I let out a wail of misery.

'No!' Luka shouted in my head.

It felt like she'd reached into my stomach and lit a match inside of me. Everything burned and I wanted to die.

"You lie." She looked uncertain now.

"I'm the only one … he can … feed from." Words were hard to find because I was freaking the hell out. There was a knife sticking so far inside me that I was sure it went through to my back. I'd never felt pain like this. Sweat broke out onto my skin as I fought to stay conscious. "You just … killed him," I rasped.

She let go of the handle and stumbled backward as I peered down to see it sticking out of my stomach. It was so low you would have thought she'd aimed to cut out my vagina. She'd likely stabbed me right in the uterus.

Bitch.

The door blew off its hinges and then Luka was before us, taking in the entire scene with wild eyes.

"What have you done!?" he screamed when he saw me and the knife embedded in my gut. In a blur he zoomed over to the two male vampires who'd just stood and watched Cassara try to kill me and ripped both of their heads off with his bare hands in seconds. I winced as they hit the floor with a dull thud.

Cassara shook her head, putting her hands out before her. "She lies. You … you can't be bonded."

When Luka's eyes went from my abdomen to the blood on Cassara's hand, chills rose up my arms. I'd never seen him look so feral. "We're more than bonded. *I love her.*" He strode across the space and pulled a stake from his waistband. "And so long as you live, you will be a threat to her."

Her eyes widened. "Lukie … you wouldn't dare. I'm the queen. She's trash. Human *fucking* trash!"

"She's my bonded feeder. By attempting to kill her, you've attempted to kill me," he sneered. "I hereby sentence you to death as a traitor."

She gasped in shock, retreating backward.

He moved so fast I barely saw him. One second Cassara was talking and the next she started to fall backward, a stake directly through her heart as she withered into an ashy husk of nothingness.

Holy shit...

Luka zoomed over to me and hooked his arms under my head, ripping the bindings off my hands.

Everything hurt, my vagina felt like it had been run over by a car, and my shoulder still throbbed from my healing bullet hole, but I couldn't get one thing out of my head: "You love me?" I said, remembering his declaration to Cassara.

He nodded. "I do. Now please don't die."

Over the next five minutes I whimpered and shook in pain as he threw me into a helicopter and I was flown somewhere nearby. It had to be nearby, because after only a few minutes at the most, we were landing. I was pulled from the helicopter and placed onto a stretcher, fading in and out of consciousness.

It was the same doctor who had operated on me before, when I got injured in Portland. The werewolf one.

"We've got to stop meeting like this," I told him through chattering teeth as my body convulsed.

The doctor shook his head. "Hang an IV, give her morphine, and prep the OR! She's going into shock."

Luka ran alongside the stretcher, his hand in mine, his eyes never leaving me.

"Aspen," he croaked.

I looked up at him.

"It's good that if you die, I die too, because I've

come to realize I can't live without you." He stroked my cheek as they fitted a mask over my face.

It was the last thing I heard before the sweet smell of sleeping gas lulled the pain and invaded my mind, turning it into mush.

All I could think was … what a beautiful way to die.

Liv's voice was the first I heard. "Will she still be able to have children?"

"She won't be able to carry them," the doctor's voice called back to Liv, "but I was able to freeze two good looking eggs from her ovaries before I had to do the operation." Shock bolted through my system. I felt woozy, tired, and confused, but those words made the morphine effects chase away in an instant.

"What's happening?" My voice was warbled and I opened my eyes to see Luka's face zoom in front of me. The look of relief that came over him melted my heart a little and I was reminded of his words.

I love her.

The doctor cleared his throat and then his face swam into view, along with Liv and my mother.

"Aspen, we are so glad to see you awake," the doctor said.

"Why are we talking about freezing my eggs?" I asked, "Stop the morphine. I can't think straight." I shook my head, panic seizing me.

The doctor nodded and reached over to place a blue clip in my IV line, pinching it shut.

"Aspen, due to the extensive damage done by the stabbing incident—"

"Just tell me!" I sobbed.

He nodded. "I had to do a full hysterectomy. You will not be able to carry your own children. I also had to take your ovaries as their blood flow was compromised, but we have a state of the art fertility department here. My colleague was able to pull two intact eggs off of the ovary that I harvested. It gives you a shot at two children if you have a surrogate and do IVF."

Holy shit. My head swam with this information. My hands went to my bandaged belly.

I'd never carry a baby? It was the *one thing* I'd wanted since I was a little girl. To be a mom, to be pregnant. Two kids, white picket fence.

A sob ripped from my throat, but then I cried out in pain because it only caused my stomach to contract.

"I'll carry your future baby. My uterus is totally

perfect," Liv declared, tears running down her face.

My tears turned into laughter, which turned into more pain. "You gotta brag about your perfect uterus so soon?" I asked her.

Liv smiled.

"Marry me," Luka declared, and my whole body froze with shock.

I must not have heard him right, too much morphine still in my system. My gaze flicked to the others, and they too stood there like statues.

Oh.

I finally found my voice. "What?"

"I want you. All of you. *Forever.*" His eyes burned yellow as he reached up and grasped the back of my neck. "You're stuck with me forever anyway. You might as well get some perks out of the relationship." He grinned.

My cheeks burned and I swallowed hard. Was he seriously asking me to marry him? His late wife's body was barely ash and he was already moving on? To be fair, she was never his wife, she was a business arrangement.

Footsteps retreated as my mother and Liv and the doctor left so we'd be alone.

"Luka. You're not thinking clearly." What he asked, the commitment he was throwing out there, was no casual thing. It was what I wanted from Sterling for so long.

Luka's brows knotted together. "I've never been more clearheaded. I know what I want, Aspen. I'm in love with you and I want you to be my wife."

Shock ripped through my system at his boldness and surety. He was dead serious, and I allowed myself to have some bit of hope that this could be real.

"But … don't you need to marry a vampire? What will the council say?"

"Screw the council, Aspen! I'll do as I please," he roared. "Are you saying no?" His hand dropped away from me, hurt running across his face.

I smiled, letting a full-fledged grin light up my face. "I'm in love with you too, and my answer is hell yes."

"Dammit, woman, you almost gave me a heart attack." Stepping closer, he bent down and pressed his nose to mine. "My wife is dead and you're technically my fiancée. Does this mean I get a kiss?"

I was in pain, exhausted, and totally not looking super-hot, but I couldn't help but beam at him. Lifting my chin, I brushed my lips against his. He reached up and traced his fingers across my neck, sending a shiver down my spine.

After a moment, I pulled back, still processing the news from the doctor.

"What if I can't have kids? What if the two eggs don't take?" It was a little early to be talking about kids—he'd only just proposed—but I knew having heirs was important for him, especially as a king. I didn't know much about IVF, but I knew it could take multiple rounds, and that was assuming I had enough fey in my system to even have a child with him. I wasn't sure how all of that worked.

"I don't care about any of that, Aspen. I want you in whatever package you come in."

My throat tightened. "But—"

"I'd rather lose my kingdom than you." He stroked my hand. "They took my mother and my sister from me, but they won't take you."

My throat tightened and I nodded. How did I get so lucky?

"Rest." He leaned forward and kissed my forehead, reaching out to pull the blue clip off the morphine line. I nodded, laying my head back, heaviness pulling at my eyelids, and then I fell into a deep, peaceful sleep.

OVER THE NEXT week I was nursed back to heath by Liv, my mom, and Luka. Maple helped a little when she could be pulled away from the TV. She was learning about the outside world through Netflix, which was a dangerous thing, but we were all just focused on letting her live an innocent childhood and not get caught up in the dangers of life yet.

Luka only fed every two days in order to give me the best chance to fully heal. The doctor had done a great job, and with my slightly advanced fey healing I was already walking around and eighty percent back to normal. My shoulder was completely healed, and other than being unable to work out or do sit ups, my stomach felt fine as well.

Liv, Sage, Demi, and I all stood around the kitchen island, snacking. The girls had stopped by to check on my healing.

Demi wagged her eyebrows. "Luka went ring shopping with Sawyer yesterday."

Sage reached out and smacked Demi's arm. "You aren't supposed to tell her!"

I grinned in excitement.

Luka was informing the elder vampire council of his intent to marry me today, but only *after* our hearing with the Magical Creature Council. Cassara's parents had filed a complaint with the Magical Creature Council. Now Luka needed to prove he'd killed his wife, the vampire queen, with good reason.

"I'm nervous to meet the memory witch. Does it hurt?" I asked Demi. Luka had told me that the council had a witch who could play your memories out for everyone to see and that's how they prosecuted crimes. I was a witness in Cassara's murder investigation, so my memory testimony would be heard. Luka had told me that Demi had previously been through the process and I was curious to hear her thoughts.

"Not physically." A darkness passed over her face, and I knew there was a story there, but she'd share it when and if she was ready.

Nerves started to tighten my gut. "You think they'll put him back in prison?"

"They can't. He's immune from crimes at this point, but they *could* take his crown and then charge him if they wanted to work around the law. I don't think they will though. Luka said it was all by the book."

That was true, he *had* stated Cassara was guilty of treason before he killed her, but I was still nervous.

"So wedding in three days?" Liv changed the subject, which I was grateful for. I wanted to focus on the positive.

I grinned. "Luka doesn't want to wait." I was sure

some of that had to do with me pledging to be a virgin until marriage, and him needing a wife to remain king. Either way, I didn't care, commitment was never my problem. I loved Luka and I couldn't wait to spend the rest of my life with him.

"What if the council says you can't be his wife because you're not a vamp?" Sage asked, and then hissed as Demi stomped on her foot.

"Sorry," Sage offered.

"No, it's okay … we marry in three days, no matter what the council says." I tipped my chin up proudly.

Demi smiled, but it didn't reach her eyes. I knew she was happy for Luka and I, but also probably worried for the alliance if Luka was unseated as king.

Not to mention the issue we'd have of Ruby and her people staying here if Luka lost his crown. She'd called and said she'd hit a delay, but that she and the House of Thorns would be here tomorrow.

There was a knock at the door and I jumped up, crossing the room quickly. Luka stood there in a crisp black suit, looking as handsome as ever. "Oh crap, should I dress up for this or something?" I looked down at my jean shorts and tank-top with ass-kicker boots.

Luka stepped forward, reaching out to grasp the

back of my neck, and pulled my lips to his. Warmth spread throughout my limbs and I grinned.

"I love that I can kiss you whenever I want now," he purred in my ear. "You look beautiful. No need to dress up."

I swallowed hard, looking behind me to see my three friends giggling and grinning ear to ear.

"Be back soon!" I said nervously, and waved them off.

Luka led me out the door, and it closed behind us. "I was thinking, when we get married and you move into the main castle with me, maybe your mom and sister could take over the guest house permanently."

I stopped, looking over at him with tears in my eyes. "Seriously?"

He nodded. "If they want. If *you* want."

I bobbed my head up and down eagerly. "I want."

A grin tugged at his lips and he pulled something from his pocket. Grasping my left hand, he slipped something onto my ring finger and I grinned. I gasped when I saw the pear-shaped red ruby. "It matches your hair." He winked.

A red ring. It was so fitting for me. I wasn't like other girls, I didn't want that white diamond princess cut stuff. This was … perfect.

"I love it." Stepping onto my tip toes, I pressed a kiss to his cheek.

Holy crap, I was engaged to be married! It was everything I'd wanted. Commitment, a lifelong promise, devotion. I never in a million years thought Luka would be the one to give it to me. I was glad it was him. He'd changed my entire way of thinking.

"Anything I should know about the Magical Creature Council? About the truth witch lady?" We continued our walk to the main castle.

He nodded. "She will see everything. You can't hide anything from her, so don't bother trying to lie."

Okay. I wasn't going to, but good to have a warning about that. Before I knew it, we were entering the castle. The guards all bowed low to Luka, which was incredibly weird—and also a little sexy that my man had so much power.

We came upon a room that had two open double doors with a vampire guard at each side. Again they bowed, and Luka took my hand into his and waltzed inside like he owned the place.

The second we entered, my eyes flitted about the room, taking in its occupants. Along the far wall sat the elder vampires. They leaned back casually in their high-backed chairs and stared at us with unreadable expressions.

Standing front and center in the room was a

female witch. She wore a black cloak and had long, silky, dark hair that cascaded over one shoulder. Her dark cherry red lips were pursed as she looked at Luka and I, but when I got to her eyes, I saw a kindness there.

"King Drake." She bowed her head slightly in respect.

Luka tipped his head back to her. "Where is the rest of the council?"

"Dealing with another issue. Today I am your judge, jury, and possible executioner." If not for a playfulness in her tone, I would have pissed myself. How could she joke about a thing like this?

He extended his hand. "I assure you, I've done nothing wrong."

She raised an eyebrow. "Eager."

"I have more pressing matters to meet with my elder council about," he informed her.

I blushed. He was talking about us getting married.

"I see." She nodded curtly. "Please unclasp your hands so I can read you one at a time. I would like to read the lady first."

Nervous energy thrummed throughout my body, but I nodded.

Dropping Luka's hand, I reached out to the woman. I flinched, every muscle in my body preparing to be electrocuted, but when our skin touched there was no pain. The moment she took my hand, I felt a presence invade my mind. It was the weirdest thing. It was like my brain was pinched tightly for a second, and then a slithering feeling slipped through it.

"Show me the night Cassara Drake was killed," she commanded.

My thoughts went to the night Cassara slipped into my bedroom and roused me from sleep, and then suddenly the far wall lit up with the images. It showed me in the bed, Cassara with her hand over my mouth. I gasped at the shock of seeing my own memories played out like a movie.

"Wake up, little bitch," Cassara's voice echoed throughout the room and the elders shifted nervously in their seats. I swallowed hard, a shiver running down my back. She cracked me over the head and then the screen went black for a moment. Next to me, Luka growled possessively.

The wall then opened up to the scene in the castle room where Cassara had me tied to the chair. I whimpered as she drove the knife into my gut after I'd confessed being bonded to Luka.

"Bonded!" one of the elders shouted to us.

Crap. I hadn't thought about that secret coming out here.

'Don't worry,' was all Luka told me.

Staring at a moving image of yourself with a knife sticking out of your own gut was beyond traumatizing, but then the scene shifted to where Luka barged in.

"She's my bonded feeder," Luka's voice rang out from the movie screen, "By attempting to kill her, you've attempted to kill me. I hereby sentence you to death as a traitor."

I winced at the gruesome scene of Luka killing Cassara all over again.

The screen faded and the witch released my hand. "Thank you, Aspen." There was a kindness to her voice, as if we'd shared something intimate and she was respectful of that.

I liked her.

Holding her hand out to Luka, she looked at the elders. "I will make sure their versions align. That no magic was involved to trick me."

They just nodded.

Rather than the scene play out again, the witch just peered at Luka, her eyes going glassy. Her brow furrowed and mouth turned down before lifting back up. It was as if she was living through a lifetime of memories in that one moment. Tears lined her eyes and I suddenly knew she was looking into more than just that night with Cassara. I wanted to know what she saw. Was it true Luka killed his own father? Had he been there when his sister and mom died? I wanted to know it all and I didn't. After a moment, she dropped Luka's hand and blinked back tears.

"Thank you, King Drake." Her voice was filled with emotion.

He cleared his throat, as if he were suddenly emotional as well.

The witch turned to address the vampire elders. "In the case of Cassara Drake's murder, the Magical Creature Council finds no wrongdoing in the actions of Luka Drake, and will not be pursuing this matter further."

I sagged in relief as the witch tipped her head to the council and then turned, stepping toward me.

Lowering her voice, she whispered. "I saw what you did in the breeder encampment."

I froze.

Crap. Here to absolve Luka of one crime, was she about to commit me for another?

"Well done," she murmured.

Surprise ran through me as she grinned and turned on her heel to leave.

Okay … that chick was *not* what I expected.

Luka stepped over to me and kissed the top of my hand. "Wait for me outside?"

I nodded.

He was about to ask the elders' permission to marry a human. Obviously he would want to do so privately. Well, technically I was an Ithaki fey-human, but I might as well be human.

I walked away from him and crossed the room in long strides, stepping out of the double doors as the two guards closed them. I didn't want to be tempted to eavesdrop, so I walked all the way down the hallway and out into the courtyard, where I sat on a stone bench.

It was beautiful in this garden. The white jasmine grew up the stone wall, encompassing the garden, and when the wind passed by, it brought the fragrance from the petals to my nose.

"WE CAN MARRY." Luka's voice made me jump. "I will keep my title, and you will be honored as queen and my wife … under one condition." His words thrummed excitement through me.

That was a fast verdict.

"Anything," I told him, standing and throwing my arms around his neck, grinning ear to ear.

The absolute look of dread on his face made the smile slip from my mouth.

"What is it?" My voice shook.

"I … have to change you into a vampire."

I gasped, stumbling away from him as his statement shook my very core.

No. Not that. I couldn't do that.

"I'm sorry, Luka, I…"

He nodded. "I would never ask you to."

Relief rushed through me.

"Not to mention, it would kill you, as I would no longer be your feeder," I reminded him.

Luka chewed the inside of his lip. "Actually, the elders have assured me that this is the only way to break the bond. In the instance you become a vampire, we are both absolved from the bond and can feed from whomever we want."

"How can they know that?" I was shocked; guilt gnawed at me. I could marry him, let him keep his crown, *and* break our very inconvenient bond?

"They have records of a few past cases of bonding," was all he said. His face was so devoid of emotion, I couldn't read him.

"What happens if you marry me now? As I am," I asked.

"They'll give me a month to remain as king."

"Then what?" I pressed him.

His face fell. "Then Morgana will take the title."

No. I couldn't allow that.

"But… she won't honor your alliance with the wolves."

Luka sighed. "I don't want to think about that right now, okay? It won't be my problem anymore. I've done what I intended to do as king. I just want to marry you. I deserve a happy ever after."

He did. So did I.

I gave it a second thought. Becoming a vampire. Dying. No heartbeat. Drinking blood. But it was all too much for me to consider. I just couldn't go that far for love, and I felt awful for it, but God made me human and I wanted to stay that way.

I dipped my chin, staring at the ground in shame. "Luka, I'm sorry I—"

Luka reached out and grasped my chin, forcing me to look up at him. "My mother wanted a better life for my sister and I. She taught us the beauty in a frail human existence with an expiration date. I never wanted to become a vampire, and I wouldn't want that for you."

"But … you will have to give all of this up." I looked around the opulent castle grounds.

He grinned. "So what? I'll have you. That's all I need."

The perfectness of his words were too much. Stepping forward, I rested my head on his chest as he held me. He never spoke about his mother, and now that he was in a sharing mood, I wanted to ask something that had been weighing on me.

"Luka … is it true you killed your father?" I looked up at him and watched as a cold darkness washed over his features. His body bristled against mine.

"Yes," he growled.

"I'm sorry," I rushed. "I didn't mean to blurt it out like that, and you don't need to tell me about it. I just had heard and—"

He shook his head, cutting me off. "If you're going to marry me, you should know everything."

I nodded, and he led me over to the stone bench, where we both sat.

"I haven't thought about this in a long time." He rubbed the back of his neck.

I reached out to stroke his arm encouragingly.

"My dad was a vampire before he met my mom. He was a Drake, so he had his sperm frozen before he was changed."

I just dipped my head in understanding, although that was so weird to me.

"My mom wanted to experience childbirth herself. Instead of getting a human surrogate. When they got married, my father agreed that after two heirs she would be *changed*."

Changed. Into a freaking vampire. The way he said it was so casual, it was weird.

"Well…" Luka looked off at a pale yellow rose

bush. "She said the day I was born changed everything for her. She saw the meaning of life, she found her purpose, she realized that she wanted to remain human, and that being a vampire for the sake of keeping a royal line pure was unnatural."

I gasped and he nodded. "It was scandalous thinking. My dad lost it, threatened to divorce her, but she was from a very reputable vampire family. The Bloodstones, old money, bankers and politicians."

Bankers. *I'd have to tell Liv so she could snag one,* I thought.

I stroked his arm. "What happened?"

Luka shrugged. "When I was twelve years old, they got into a big fight in the kitchen. My little sister was ten. My dad … threatened to change my mom against her will."

I gasped. It sounded like rape. Worse even, if that was possible.

Luka's face drew back in a pained expression. "I always respected my dad. He was tough on us and traveled a lot, but he was decent, and for all their arguing, he never hit my mom. Until that night."

A single tear rolled down my cheek. The pain of his story bled throughout our bond and wrapped around us both.

"He tried to change her right there in the middle

of the kitchen, but she was a fearsome woman. Trained at birth as all Bloodstone women are. Trained to be a warrior, a queen. She fought him and … he killed her."

Holy crap.

And he saw all that? As a twelve-year-old boy?

"Luka, I'm so sorry."

"So I killed him," he growled. "With his back turned, I took his head clean off and avenged my beloved mother."

A somber mood fell over the both of us. I would have absolutely done the same thing. He was so deep in the memory I didn't dare say anything to pull him out.

"My aunt Morgana took us in. She allowed Nico to change my sister against her will at age eighteen, but she died in the process because he did it wrong. Then Morgana changed me against my will after forcing me to officially sign the betrothal papers with Cassara's family." Luka turned to face me. There was a storm in his eyes. They were nearly black, his jaw clenched shut and his chest shaking slightly. "There you have it, Aspen, all of my darkness laid bare for you to see. I understand if you don't want to sleep next to me every night knowing what I've done."

His head dipped down in shame and I laughed. It

caught him off guard and he jerked up to look at me, confused.

"Are you kidding me? I feel better now knowing the story. If anyone kills me, you're totally going to avenge me. They say a man treats his wife as he treats his mother." I smiled playfully.

"I absolutely would avenge you." His voice was dead serious.

Leaning forward, I trailed my fingers down his temple. "Luka, I was awful to you from the first day we met. I said horrible things and treated you like a demon. As far as I'm concerned, you're a better person than me."

"Not possible, my love," he assured me, twisting a lock of my red hair. "But probably a close second."

Laughter bubbled out of me and he stood, picking me up into his arms as I squealed in delight. "I'm gonna marry this woman!" he shouted into the empty garden, causing more laughter to peal out of me. Looking down at me in his arms, his eyes glowed like the embers of a dying fire. "I love you, Aspen Rose."

Reaching up, I ran my fingers through his hair. "I love you too."

As he leaned in to kiss me, I had a single thought: when I got old and died, he would die too because of our feeder bond. Was that wrong? Or was that what he wanted all along when he'd said he wanted to remain human? I should have probably considered the vampire thing longer, at least give it ten seconds of thought, but the mere idea revolted me. To be undead, to cease breathing, to drink blood to sustain life. It wasn't natural. I couldn't do it, not even for him.

I pulled away from him and met his gaze. "I'm sorry I can't—"

"Stop it," he said. "It was an impossible thing to ask. Besides, I kind of like that we have this limited time together. It makes each day something to cherish."

I nodded. "Are you still going to be attracted to me when I'm like a fifty-year-old lady?" I scrunched up my face.

Luka grinned. "You'll be a sexy little cougar, I have no doubt."

More laughter. I was always laughing with him and I couldn't wait to spend the rest of my life with him. However short it might be in vampire years.

"Go on a date with me," Luka exclaimed. "Tonight."

"A date?" I raised my eyebrows.

Luka nodded. "Yeah, you know that thing normal people do before they get engaged."

I chuckled. "Okay. A date."

Setting me down, we walked hand and hand back to the guest cottage. "I'll pick you up at six."

"Perfect." I kissed him and slipped inside, completely floating on top of my love cloud. Luka gave me everything I desired in a relationship and more.

SAGE, Demi and Liv all sat around the dining table as my mom made us lunch. My half sis was glued to the TV as usual.

"Her brain is going to explode." Liv peered through the entry to the dining room out into the living room, where Maple stared at the TV.

I giggled. "She asked me for a cell phone and when she'd be old enough to drive."

We all burst into snickers. "Learning life through the Kardashians is dangerous," Demi exclaimed.

"What's a Kardashian?" Sage looked confused.

This just made us laugh harder.

"I'll slowly wean her off. Get her some good books. Do they have a library in Vampire City?" I mused.

Demi grinned. "Nope, but that can be your first contribution as queen."

My face fell and they all noticed. I'd only just gotten back from the hearing and I was avoiding having to talk about it other than to tell them Luka was absolved of Cassara's murder. I'd shown them the ring and they all just assumed that part went okay.

Demi's eyes sharpened. "The elders said it was cool you guys marry, right?"

I didn't say anything. I was trying to find the words, knowing I'd let her down.

"Oh my God, you *can* marry, right?" Liv blurted out.

I nodded. "We can … but in order for Luka to remain king, they wanted one thing … one thing neither of us is comfortable with."

Sage clutched her chest. "Your firstborn!"

I snorted. "No. For him to change me into a vampire."

"They didn't!" Demi slammed her fist on the table and the wood creaked.

"Shhhh. I don't want to tell my mom," I hissed, and peered into the kitchen where she was stirring something in a pot. She looked back at me but I waved her off.

"How dare they!" Demi whisper-screamed. "Not to mention it's fucking illegal to change a human!"

"Well, I'm not exactly human, am I?"

"So what now? If you marry, he's no longer king?"

I nodded. "It would go to Morgana."

"Well, screw that. She's a psycho," Sage interjected.

Silence fell over the table and I suddenly felt like the weight of the world was pressing on my shoulders. Demi picked at her fingernails nervously. I knew she must be thinking about how this would affect the werewolves and the fragile alliance.

"Demi, I'm so sorry," I sobbed, reaching for her hand.

She grasped mine and looked into my eyes, her bright blue irises flaring yellow. "Don't you dare be sorry. Drinking blood is gross as hell, I wouldn't want to become a bloodsucker either. Besides, if we're talking supernaturals, you'd make a cuter werewolf." She winked.

I laughed, wiping my tears. "I'm staying human-ish, but thank you for the offer."

Demi squeezed my hand. "Sawyer and I will figure it out. We always do."

I nodded, pulling my hand back, but her reassurance did little to ease the guilt inside of me.

Our lunch was a silent one, everyone lost in their own thoughts. My mom had made some yummy spicy rice and bean dish that was common in her encampment. She'd served it with fresh handmade tortillas as well. The girls stayed for an hour and then took off, telling us they would be back in two days for the wedding.

When I shut the door, I leaned my head against the cool wood and sighed. What a day. Liv's arm draped around me.

"You can't feel guilty for this. I won't allow it," she declared.

I gave her a small smile. It was hard knowing that you could fix everything if you made a certain choice, but that choice was just taking it too far for me.

"I'm going to lie down and then get ready for my date with Luka," I told her.

She nodded, but I could see the concern in her gaze. "Let me know if you want help doing your hair."

I gave her a thumbs-up and then went back to my room to be alone and feel sorry for myself.

AFTER STARING at the ceiling for a good two hours, I showered and got ready for my date with my fiancé. The word *fiancé* just made me grin, as did the giant ruby ring on my finger.

Speaking of Ruby…

My phone buzzed with a text.

Ruby: Still all good to come there tomorrow morning? Sixty-seven of us total.

I'd had a talk with Luka yesterday. He was already setting up a makeshift disaster shelter, which was basically a giant barn with bunkbeds and sleeping bags and porta potties. It would be good enough for now until we could find a more permanent solution. I was hoping that solution was that we killed Maz and could all return back to Spokane safely. Especially now that Luka would lose his crown.

Me: All good. Ready for you.

I sent back and closed my phone before noticing it was dying.

Dang it.

I'd left my charger in my car when I'd taken it to Spokane. I hadn't been sure if Liv and I were going to stay the night or not, so I'd packed a bag and left it in there.

I had time before Luka arrived, and some fresh air would be nice anyway.

Slipping out the front door, I crossed the pathway that led from our little guest cottage and wound down to the front of the castle to the main parking lot.

The sun was setting and the lights kicked on, illuminating my little yellow Beetle. Man, I loved that car. It was one of the first things I'd bought myself with my bounty hunter money.

Reaching up, I rubbed the healing scar over my arm where Maz had shot me.

A Munai.

I hadn't really allowed myself to process all that with her. It was too traumatic. Not only had she lied to us our whole life, she wasn't even human herself.

Unlocking the door, I reached into the back seat and pulled out my duffle bag. Luka's black Range Rover pulled up behind my Beetle and I smiled. As the window rolled down, I waved to him, about to tell him I was going to run my duffle bag inside first, when I realized I didn't recognize the driver. There was movement behind me and a hand clamped around my mouth. Before I could process anything, I was being pushed with force toward the Range Rover, dropping my duffle on the floor. The back door opened and I was tossed in kicking and screaming. I landed hard on my side, a slight pain throbbing in my healing gut before the door slammed and then the tires squealed.

I was thrown backward even further in the seat as the car took off like a rocket. Before I could get my bearings, a gun cocked and then cold metal was pressed against my temple. I froze, my eyes adjusting to the dimness of the vehicle.

Morgana.

I was sprawled out in the back seat while she sat shotgun, a Glock aimed at my forehead.

'Luka, help. I've been kidnapped ... again. Morgana. Leaving the parking lot in a black Range Rover,' I rushed out.

"I heard a little rumor," Morgana purred. "That you are Luka's bonded feeder. Is this true?" She grinned like the confirmation of this news would bring her great joy.

'Luka!' I screamed, panicking that he wasn't responding.

"She's trying to mentally contact him," the driver said, and my throat went bone dry.

"So it's true!" Morgana looked pleased, continuing to aim the pistol at me as the car wove in and out of the parking lot.

'Luka!' Desperation gripped me.

"Oh, honey, he's blocking you." She pointed at the driver. "He's a very powerful warlock. Luka has no idea where you are, and he won't until you're dead."

Ice cold fear trickled down my veins and settled in my gut.

Note to self: stop getting kidnapped.

"Where are you taking me?" My gaze darted

around the car, trying to map out exits or identify weapons I could use before she put a bullet in my brain. The only thing I had were my stiletto boots with tiny stakes at the tip. I'd been going out on a date night, not a hunting raid. I hadn't expected to need to be fully armed.

The car rolled onto some gravel and then pulled to a stop as the door flew open.

"Here." Morgana grinned as a man yanked me out by my armpits. It scared me how fast they were moving, how little she was talking. How much she looked like she wanted to kill me.

"Hey!" I bucked in his arms, cracking my head backward into the face of whoever held me, and then pulled the caps off my stilettos.

"Don't." Morgana's voice came from behind me, and that damn gun was pressed between my shoulder blades.

The dude who held me released his grip and walked over to the car, slipping inside. Did he freaking run alongside the vehicle the entire time? Where the hell had he come from?

This was all happening too fast.

I looked around frantically, and my heart sank into my stomach. We were in a wooded strip of land off the main road. A place you went to kill someone.

She was going to kill me, and therefore starve Luka so they would crown her queen.

"You're a coward." I tried to bait her into conversation.

It worked.

"Excuse me?" The gun released from my back and she walked around to face me.

"Killing Luka this way. *Coward.*"

Morgana grinned. "I'm not killing Luka, *that* is against vampire law now that he is King. I'm killing you."

I didn't know what I expected to happen. Maybe that she would talk some more, or at least get closer so that I could heel kick her in the face, but when the muzzle of the gun flared with light and pain licked into my stomach, my mouth opened in shock.

Not again.

First Maz shoots me.

Then Cassara cuts out my womb … and now this? I flew backward as she unloaded the entire clip into my stomach. I hit the ground hard, butt first, flying onto my back. Sharp, deep, and pulsating pain burned in my stomach and I opened my mouth to scream but nothing came out.

"Goodbye." Morgana waved playfully before getting into the SUV and driving off, spitting dust and gravel up in my face.

I grasped my stomach, feeling the sticky wet blood pool around me as dizziness washed over me.

'Aspen!' Luka's bloodcurdling scream ripped through my head the second the warlock was far enough away from me, seemingly no longer blocking my bond. I couldn't even think clear enough to respond to him at first. *'I saw your duffle bag in the parking lot and I can't find you, but I feel you close.'*

There were so many holes. I probed them with my fingers as my chest rattled with each breath.

Liv, my mom, Maple, Luka, Sterling, even Vasquez, they all flooded my mind then in a montage of images and memories. Tears streamed down my face.

I'd had a beautiful life. It was hard at times, and I made some questionable choices, but damn it was good.

'I loved you so much ... I need you to know that,' I thought to Luka.

"I'm here!" His voice echoed farther down the road. "Aspen, call to me! I smell you."

I took in another deep breath to cry out to him, but my chest rattled so hard I just coughed.

"ASPEN!" Luka's face swam into view then as he skidded to a stop, slipping on the gravel road and falling before me. I would never forget the heartbreak and horror etched in his beautiful features. The way he looked from my abdomen to my face and the resignation that washed over us both.

"It's… o… kay." I reached up with wet, sticky fingers and grasped his cheek. "I'm… ready… to…" A cough wracked my chest before I could finish speaking. "…go." I wheezed and suddenly I felt weightless, like my earthly body could no longer contain my soul. I was flying, lifting up into the air.

There's no pain here, I thought. *I feel so free.*

'Well, I'm not ready to let you go!' Luka invaded my thoughts and then pain sliced along my wrist. I slammed back into my body and my eyelids flew open.

What the…?

Luka was feeding from me. Why?

Unless…

"No," I whimpered. "I don't… want to… be like… you," I wheezed as Luka pulled away from my wrist and then brought his own over to my mouth. His face was ashen, shocked, and pulled taut, eyes wild.

"Drink," he commanded, drawing a sharp nail across his wrist.

The second the salty, coppery blood hit my tongue, I recoiled. "No! Luka… let me go. I want to be… with God."

He bit on his lip, but a sob ripped from his throat. "I can't."

With his other hand, he pried my jaw open and then squeezed his blood into my mouth. The thick crimson fluid trickled down my tongue and I coughed, trying to throw it up. This wasn't right, this wasn't natural. I wanted to stay the way I was. The way God intended me to be. After everything Luka had said he went through with being changed against his will, he was doing the same to me?

'Please don't. I'll never forgive you,' I whimpered.

His hand yanked away from my jaw then and it snapped shut. He pulled his wrist from my mouth and stared at me with a brokenness that tore my heart in two.

"You seriously can't be asking me to let you die…" His chest heaved as he pulled himself closer to me and nuzzled my neck, breaking into sobs.

That light feeling was back, the one where I felt like I was about to float away. It was a safe feeling. There was comfort in letting go of this painful, earthly body.

'You were... so... good to me,' I rasped. *'Thank you.'*

"Change her!" a familiar voice commanded, and then Liv stepped into view, hovering over me. She was holding a stake. "Right. Fucking. *Now.*"

Luka froze against my neck, looking up at Liv. "I can't," he breathed. "I won't."

Liv fell at my knees, weeping. "Aspen, you idiot! You have to kill Maz and save all of the mothers and children in the other breeder camps. You have to keep the werewolf and vampire peace accord. You have to get married, and have babies, and we have to move to our island." Her sobs cut right into my soul, and a flicker of fight flared up inside of me. Liv beat on the ground. "You have too much to do!"

She was right. This wasn't about me. Without me, Luka would be dead in two days, which meant Ruby and all her people were walking into a Morgana trap. She'd kill them all, and with them would die the only hope of saving the other breeders.

Looking over at Luka, I nodded once, the coldness starting to settle into my bones as my soul felt barely tethered to my body.

"Do it," I croaked with what little breath I had left.

Luka was a blur of movement, slicing his arm and holding it over my mouth. I drank and drank and drank until I wanted to vomit, but somehow I kept it down. Finally, when I was full of Luka's blood, the tether to my body snapped and I died with a smile on my face.

<hr>

I WAS FLOATING in a tunnel of white light. It wasn't like any light I'd ever seen before. I could hear the light, feel the light, smell the light—I *was* the light. The light was a being in and of itself, and it wrapped me into its sweet embrace, taking away all of my pain and sorrow. I just lay there in my little light cocoon for some time until I felt a tug at my navel.

'*Come back.*' Luka's voice pierced the light as it started to tear apart and splinter. '*Come back.*'

'*No,*' I whimpered.

I wanted to stay in the light forever. There was no pain here, no heaviness or grief. Before I could even say goodbye to it, there was a yank, and then I dropped like a stone back into my body.

My eyelids flung open and I sat up with a scream.

PREORDER BOOK THREE **the final book in the Vampire Hunter Society series!**

THE DARK SOUL · BOOK 3
VAMPIRE
HUNTER SOCIETY
USA TODAY BESTSELLING AUTHOR
LEIA STONE